Penguin Books
The Lost Honour of Katharina Blum

Heinrich Böll was born in Cologne in 1917. The son of a sculptor, he began work in a bookshop, then served in the infantry throughout the war. After 1945 he took various jobs, becoming a freelance writer in 1951. He has since worked as a novelist, short-story writer and radio playwright. His first novels, *The Train Was on Time* and *And Where Were You, Adam?*, concerned the despair of those involved in total war; his later works, including *Acquainted with the Night* and *The Unguarded House*, deal with the moral vacuum behind the post-war 'economic miracle' in Western Germany, and *The Bread of Those Early Years* depicts the poverty, the greyness and the continual hunger of the period shortly after the war. In his short-story writing Böll is regarded as one of the founders of the contemporary German American-style *Kurzgeschichte*. Among his other novels are *And Never Said a Word* (1952), *End of a Mission* (1968), *Group Portrait with Lady* (1973) and *Children Are Civilians Too* (1973). Heinrich Böll was elected the first Neil Gunn Fellow by the Scottish Arts Council in 1970 and was awarded the Nobel Prize for Literature in 1972. He is an outspoken defender of artistic freedom, a past president of International PEN, and has been active on behalf of Solzhenitsyn and other writers throughout the world.

Heinrich Böll

The Lost Honour of Katharina Blum

*Or: How violence develops and
where it can lead*

Translated from the German
by Leila Vennewitz

Penguin Books

Penguin Books Ltd, Harmondsworth, Middlesex, England
Penguin Books, 625 Madison Avenue, New York, New York 10022, U.S.A.
Penguin Books Australia Ltd, Ringwood, Victoria, Australia
Penguin Books Canada Ltd, 2801 John Street, Markham, Ontario, Canada L3R 1B4
Penguin Books (N.Z.) Ltd, 182–190 Wairau Road, Auckland 10, New Zealand

Die verlorene Ehre der Katharina Blum first published 1974
This translation first published in Great Britain by
Martin Secker & Warburg Ltd 1975
Published in Penguin Books 1978
Reprinted 1980, 1981

Copyright © Verlag Kiepenheuer & Witsch Köln 1974
English translation copyright © Heinrich Böll and
Leila Vennewitz, 1975
All rights reserved

Made and printed in Great Britain by
Hazell Watson & Viney Ltd, Aylesbury, Bucks
Set in Linotype Plantin

The characters and action in
this story are purely fictitious . . .

I

For the following account there are a few minor sources and three major ones; these will be named here at the beginning and not referred to again. Major sources are: the transcripts of the police interrogation; Hubert Blorna (attorney); and Peter Hach (public prosecutor, also high-school and university classmate of Hubert Blorna). It was Hach who – in confidence, needless to say – supplemented the transcripts and reported certain measures taken by the police investigators as well as the results of their inquiries absent from the transcripts: not, we hasten to add, for official purposes but solely for private use. Hach was genuinely affected by the concern and frustration suffered by his friend Blorna, who could find no explanation for the whole affair and yet, 'when I come to think about it', found it 'not inexplicable, but almost logical'. Since the case of Katharina Blum will, in any event, remain more or less fictitious, because of the attitude of the accused and the very awkward position of her defence counsel Blorna, such minor and very human lapses in conduct as those committed by Hach may be not only understandable but forgivable.

The minor sources, some of greater and some of lesser significance, need not be mentioned here, since their respective implication, involvement, relevancy, bias, bewilderment, and testimony will all emerge from this report.

2

If this report – since there is such frequent mention of sources – should at times be felt to be 'fluid', we beg the reader's forgiveness: it has been unavoidable. To speak of 'sources' and 'fluidity' is to preclude all possibility of composition, so perhaps we should instead introduce the concept of 'bringing together', of 'conduction', a concept that should be clear to anyone who as a child (or even as an adult) has ever played in, beside, or *with* puddles, draining them, linking them by channels, emptying, diverting, and rerouting them until the entire available puddlewater-potential is *brought together* in a collective channel to be diverted on to a different level or perhaps even duly rerouted in orderly fashion into the gutter or drain provided by the local authorities. The sole objective here, therefore, is to effect a kind of drainage. Clearly a due process of order! So whenever this account appears to be in a fluid state in which differences in and adjustments to level play a part, we ask the reader's indulgence, since there will always be stoppages, blockages, siltings, unsuccessful attempts at conduction, and sources 'that can never come together', not to mention subterranean streams, and so on, and so on.

3

The first facts to be presented are brutal: on Wednesday, 20 February 1974, on the eve of the traditional opening of Carnival, a young woman of twenty-seven leaves her apartment in a certain city at about 6.45 p.m. to attend a dance at a private home.

Four days later, after a dramatic – there is no getting around the word (and here we have an example of the various levels that permit the stream to flow) – turn of events, on Sunday evening at almost the same hour (to be precise, at about 7.04 p.m.) she rings the front door bell at the home of Walter Moeding, Crime Commissioner, who is at that moment engaged, for professional rather than private reasons, in disguising himself as a sheikh, and she declares to the startled Moeding that at about 12.15 noon that day she shot and killed Werner Tötges, reporter, in her apartment, and would the Commissioner kindly give instructions for her front door to be broken down and the reporter to be 'removed'; for her part, she has spent the hours between 12.15 noon and 7.00 p.m. roaming around town in search of a remorse that she has failed to find; furthermore, she requests that she be arrested, she would like to be where her 'dear Ludwig' is.

Moeding, to whom the young person is known from various interrogations and who feels a certain sympathy towards her, does not doubt her statement for a moment; he drives her in his own car to police headquarters, informs his superior, Chief Crime Commissioner Beizmenne, of the situation, has the young woman escorted to a cell, and fifteen minutes later meets Beizmenne outside her front door, where a police commando breaks down the door and finds the young woman's statement confirmed.

Let there not be too much talk about blood here, since only *necessary* differences in level are to be regarded as inevitable; we would therefore direct the reader to television and the movies and the appropriate musicals and gruesicals; if there is to be something fluid here, let it not be blood. Perhaps attention should merely be drawn to certain colour effects: the murdered Tötges was wearing an improvised sheikh costume concocted from a rather worn sheet, and the effect of a lot of blood on a lot of white is well known; a pistol is then sure to act almost like a spray gun, and since in this instance the costume was made out of a large *square of white cotton*, modern painting or stage effects would seem to be more appropriate here than drainage. So be it. Those are the facts.

4

For a time it was considered not unlikely that Adolf Schönner, press photographer, who was also found shot but not until Ash Wednesday, in a wooded area to the west of the festive city, was likewise a victim of Blum; later, however, when a certain chronological order had been established for the course of events, this 'proved to be unfounded'. A cab driver stated later that he had driven Schönner disguised as a sheikh and a young female person dressed as an Andalusian woman to this very wood. But Tötges had been shot Sunday noon, whereas Schönner had not been killed until Tuesday noon. Although it was soon discovered that the murder weapon found beside Tötges could not possibly be the weapon with which Schönner was killed, suspicion continued to rest on Blum for several hours, notably on account of motive. If she could be said to have had grounds for taking revenge on Tötges, she had at least equal grounds for taking revenge on Schönner. But the police did concede that Blum was very unlikely to have possessed two weapons. In committing her crime, Blum had gone to work with a cool intelligence; when she was asked whether she had shot Schönner too, her answer took the form of a cryptic question: 'Yes, come to think of it, why not him too?' Then, however, the police gave up suspecting her of Schönner's murder, especially since her alibi proved on examination to be virtually watertight. No one who knew Katharina Blum or who, in the course of the investigation, became acquainted with her character, doubted that, if she had murdered Schönner, she would have admitted it without equivocation. In any event, the cab driver who had driven the couple to the wood ('I'd be more inclined to describe it as kind of overgrown bushes,' he said) did not recognize Blum from photographs. 'Hell,' he said, 'these cute kids with their brown hair, between five foot five and five foot eight, age twenty-four to twenty-seven – there's a million of them during Carnival.'

In Schönner's apartment no trace was found of Blum, or of anything pointing to the Andalusian woman. Other press photographers and friends of Schönner's knew only that on Tuesday, around noon, he had left a bar frequented by reporters 'with some broad or other'.

5

One of the leading Carnival officials, a wine and champagne dealer who took pride in his successful labours to restore Carnival jollity, was manifestly relieved that it was Monday and Wednesday respectively before both deeds became known. 'A thing like that, just when the festive season's beginning – and you can forget about the Carnival spirit *and* business. If it gets out that fancy dress is being misused for criminal purposes, the whole mood's done for right there and business is ruined. That sort of thing's a real sacrilege. High spirits and a good time need trust, that's what they're built up on.'

6

The *News* behaved somewhat oddly after the murder of two of its journalists. Wild excitement! Headlines. Front page. Special editions. Death notices of gigantic proportions. As if – if there's going to be any shooting in the world at all – the murder of a journalist were something special, more important than the murder of a bank manager, bank employee, or bank robber.

It is necessary to mention this excessive attention paid by the press to the event because it applies not only to the *News*: other newspapers also treated the murder of a reporter as something wicked, terrible, well-nigh ceremonial, one might almost say as a ritual murder. There was even mention of a 'victim of his profession', and, of course, the *News* clung tenaciously to the version that Schönner had also been one of Blum's victims. Even if one is bound to admit that Tötges would probably not have been shot had he not been a reporter (but, for example, a shoemaker or a baker), the attempt should have been made to discover whether it would not have been more appropriate to speak of a death that *resulted from* a profession; for an explanation will emerge as to why someone as intelligent and cool-headed as Blum not only planned the murder but also carried it out and, at the critical moment – one which she herself had engineered – not only seized the pistol but put it to use.

7

Let us proceed at once from this lowest of all levels to higher planes. Away with the blood. Let the excitement in the press be forgotten. Katharina Blum's apartment has meanwhile been cleaned up, the ruined rugs have landed on the garbage dump, and the furniture has been wiped and put back in place: all this at the expense and on the instructions of Blorna as empowered by his friend Hach, although it is far from certain whether Blorna will be appointed official custodian.

When all is said and done, in five years this Katharina Blum has invested seventy thousand marks in cash in a self-owned apartment worth altogether a hundred thousand marks. Hence – to quote her brother, who is at present serving a minor jail sentence–'there's lots of goodies worth swiping.' But then who would be responsible for the interest and amortization on the remaining thirty thousand marks, even if a not inconsiderable increase in value is taken into account? There would be liabilities as well as assets.

Be that as it may, by now Tötges has been buried (with disproportionate pomp and ceremony, in the opinion of many). Strangely enough, Schönner's death and funeral were accorded less display and attention. Why, one may ask? Because he was not a 'victim of his profession' but more likely the victim of a *crime passionnel*? The sheikh costume is in the police vaults, likewise the pistol (an 8mm); only Blorna knows the origin of the pistol, whereas the attempts of the police and the public prosecutor's office to find this out have been fruitless.

8

Inquiries into Blum's activities during the four days in question progressed nicely enough at first, and it was only when attempts were made to gather information about the Sunday that they were brought up short.

On the Wednesday afternoon Blorna personally paid Katharina Blum two full weeks' wages at 280 marks per week, one for the current week, the other for the week to come, since he was leaving that same afternoon for a ski-ing vacation with his wife. Katharina had not only promised the Blornas, she had positively sworn that she really would take a vacation this time and enjoy herself during Carnival instead of picking up extra work, the way she had in every previous year during the festive season. She had delightedly told the Blornas that she had been invited that evening to a small private dance at the home of her godmother, friend, and confidante, Else Woltersheim, and that she was looking forward to it very much, it had been such a long time since she had had an opportunity to dance. And Mrs Blorna had said: 'Never mind, Katie, when we come back we'll give another party, then you can dance again.' For as long as she had been living in the city, i.e., for the past five or six years, Katharina had frequently complained of the lack of opportunity 'just to go dancing somewhere'. There were, she told the Blornas, those dumps where sex-starved students went looking for a free pick-up, then there were those Bohemian-type places that were too wild for her tastes, and as for those church dances, nothing would induce her to go to those.

There was no difficulty in establishing that on Wednesday afternoon Katharina had worked for a further two hours at the home of Mr and Mrs Hiepertz, where she sometimes helped out at their request. Since the Hiepertzes were also leaving town during Carnival and going to see their daughter in Lemgo, Katharina had driven the elderly couple to the station in her Volkswagen. Despite the parking problem she had insisted on accompanying them to the platform and carrying their bags. ('Not for the money, oh no, we can't offer a thing for a kindness like that, she would be very hurt,' Mrs Hiepertz explained.)

It was confirmed that the train left at 5.30 p.m. If one was prepared to allow Katharina from five to ten minutes to find her car in the midst of the early Carnival crowds, and a further twenty to twenty-five minutes to reach her suburban apartment, so that she could not have entered it until between 6.00 and 6.15 p.m., not a single minute remained unaccounted for, provided one was fair enough to grant that she must have washed, changed, and had a bite to eat, for by 7.25 p.m. she had already turned up at Miss Woltersheim's party, not in her own car but by streetcar, and she was dressed neither as a Bedouin nor as an Andalusian but merely wore a red carnation in her hair, red stockings and shoes, a high-necked blouse of honey-coloured raw silk, and a plain tweed skirt of the same colour. It may appear unimportant whether Katharina went to the party in her car or by streetcar, but it must be mentioned here because in the course of the investigation it turned out to be of considerable significance.

9

From the moment she entered the Woltersheim apartment the investigation was facilitated because from 7.25 p.m. onward Katharina was, without realizing it, under police observation. Throughout the entire evening, from 7.30 to 10.00 p.m., before leaving the apartment with him, she had danced 'exclusively and fervently', as she later stated, with one Ludwig Götten.

10

We must not forget to pay tribute at this point to Peter Hach, the public prosecutor, for it is he alone whom we have to thank for the information – bordering on police-court gossip – that Commissioner Erwin Beizmenne had the Woltersheim and Blum telephones tapped from the moment Blum left the Woltersheim apartment with Götten. This was done in a manner that may be worth mentioning: in such cases Beizmenne would call up the appropriate superior and say: 'I need my little plugs again. Two of them this time.'

11

Götten, it seems, made no calls from Katharina's apartment. At least, Hach knew of none. One thing is certain: Katharina's apartment was under strict observation, and when by 10.30 Thursday morning there had been no phone calls and

Götten had not left the apartment, Beizmenne was beginning to lose both his patience and his nerve, and a detachment of eight heavily armed police officers broke into the apartment, storming it with the most intensive precautionary measures, searched it, but found no trace of Götten, all they found being Katharina, 'looking extremely relaxed, almost happy', standing at her kitchen counter drinking coffee from a large mug and taking a bite from a slice of white bread and butter and honey. She aroused suspicion in that she did not appear surprised but rather quite composed, 'not to say triumphant'. She was wearing a green cotton housecoat embroidered with daisies, with nothing underneath, and when she was asked by Commissioner Beizmenne ('quite roughly,' she said later) what had happened to Götten, she said she didn't know when Ludwig had left the apartment: she had woken up at 9.30 a.m. and he was already gone. 'Without saying good-bye?' 'Yes.'

12

Here we should inquire into a hotly disputed question put by Beizmenne, a question repeated by Hach, withdrawn, repeated again, and again withdrawn. Blorna considers this question important because he believes that, if it was in fact asked, it was from this and only from this that Katharina's bitterness, sense of humiliation, and fury may have stemmed. Since Blorna and his wife describe Katharina as being extremely sensitive, almost prudish, in sexual matters, the mere *possibility* must be considered that Beizmenne might – in fury, too, over the disappearance of Götten, whom he thought he had in his grasp – have asked the controversial question. Beizmenne *allegedly* asked the maddeningly composed Katharina as she leaned against her counter: 'Well, did he fuck you?' whereupon Katharina apparently not only blushed but said triumphantly: 'No, I wouldn't call it that.'

It may be safely assumed that, if Beizmenne *did* ask the question, from that moment on any feelings of trust between him and Katharina were out of the question. However, the absence of any relationship of mutual trust between the two – although there is evidence to show that Beizmenne, who is said to be 'not all that bad', tried to establish such a relationship – should not be regarded as conclusive proof that he did in fact ask the fateful question. In any event, Hach, who was present when the apartment was searched, is regarded by his friends and acquaintances as 'sex-starved' and it is quite likely that such a crude idea occurred to *him* on seeing the extremely attractive Blum girl leaning so casually against her counter, and that he would have liked to ask her that very question or perform the crudely specified activity with her.

13

The apartment was then thoroughly searched, and a few objects were confiscated, notably anything in writing. Katharina Blum was permitted to get dressed in the bathroom in the presence of a woman police officer by the name of Pletzer. Even so, the bathroom door had to remain slightly ajar and was kept under the close scrutiny of two armed police officers. Katharina was permitted to take her handbag with her, and since the possibility of arrest could not be excluded she was allowed to take along her night things, toilet articles, and something to read. Her library consisted of four love stories, three detective novels, plus a biography of Napoleon and one of Queen Christina of Sweden. All these books emanated from a book club. Because she kept on asking, 'But why, why, what have I done wrong?' she was finally informed politely by Pletzer the policewoman that Ludwig Götten was a wanted man who had been nearly convicted of bank robbery and was suspected of murder and other crimes.

14

When, at about 11.25 a.m., Katharina Blum was finally taken from her apartment for questioning, it was decided not to handcuff her after all. Beizmenne had been inclined to insist on handcuffs, but after a brief dialogue between Policewoman Pletzer and Beizmenne's assistant Moeding he agreed to waive this. Since that day marked the opening of Carnival, numerous people living in the building had not gone to work or started out yet for the annual saturnalian parades, festivities, etc., so that some three dozen occupants of the ten-storey apartment building were standing around in the lobby wearing topcoats, housecoats, and bathrobes, and Schönner the press photographer was standing just in front of the elevator when Katharina Blum, walking between Beizmenne and Moeding, flanked by armed police officers, emerged from the elevator. She was photographed repeatedly from the front, from behind, and from the side, and finally – since in her shame and confusion she kept trying to hide her face and so got all tangled up with her handbag, toilet articles, and a plastic bag containing two books and writing materials – with dishevelled hair and an angry face.

15

Half an hour later, after her rights had been explained to her and she had been given a chance to freshen up a bit, the questioning began in the presence of Beizmenne, Moeding, Policewoman Pletzer, and the public prosecutors Korten and Hach. The interrogation was recorded:

My name is Katharina Brettloh, née Blum. I was born on 2 March 1947, at Gemmelsbroich in the District of Kuir. My father was Peter Blum, a miner. He died when I was six, at the age of thirty-seven, of a lung injury received during the war. After the war my father again worked in a slate quarry and was suspected of suffering from pneumoconiosis. After his death my mother had to fight for her pension because the welfare office and the miners' local could not agree. I had to start doing housework at an early age because my father was often sick, which meant reduced pay, and my mother took on a number of jobs as a cleaning woman. I had no difficulty in school, although even while I was still there I had to do a lot of housework, not only at home but also in the homes of neighbours and others living in the village, where I used to lend a hand at baking, cooking, preserving, and slaughtering. I also did a lot of housework and helped with the harvest.

After I left school in 1961 my godmother, Else Woltersheim, of Kuir, helped me to obtain a position as a maid at the Gerbers butcher shop in Kuir, where I sometimes had to help out by serving in the store too. With the aid and financial support of my godmother, Miss Woltersheim, I attended a home-economics school at Kuir where my godmother was an instructor and from which I graduated with very good grades. From 1966 to 1967 I worked as housekeeper at the all-day kindergarten attached to the Koeschler Company in neighbouring Oftersbroich, and after that I was employed as a domestic aide by Dr Kluthen, who had a medical practice in Oftersbroich, where I only stayed a year because the doctor was making more and more passes at me and his wife did not like that. I didn't like it myself. It disgusted me.

In 1968, when I was unemployed for a few weeks and helping my mother in the house and sometimes helping out at meetings and bowling sessions of the Gemmelsbroich Fife & Drum Band, my older brother Kurt introduced me to Wilhelm Brettloh, a textile worker, whom I married a few months later. We lived in Gemmelsbroich, where on weekends when there were a lot of tourists I sometimes helped in the kitchen at Kloog's restaurant, and sometimes as a waitress behind the counter. After six months I already felt an insuperable aversion to my husband. I don't wish to go into details. I left my husband and moved to town. I was divorced as the guilty party on grounds of wilful desertion and resumed my maiden name.

First I lived at Miss Woltersheim's, until after a few weeks I found a position living in as housekeeper and general help in the home of Mr Fehnern, certified accountant. Mr Fehnern made it possible for me to attend night school and adulteducation courses and to qualify as a certified housekeeper. He was very kind and very generous, and I continued to work for him after I had passed my exams. At the end of 1969 Mr Fehnern was arrested in connection with substantial tax evasions that had been discovered among large companies for which he had been working. Before he was taken away he handed me an envelope containing three months' salary and asked me to continue looking after things; he would soon be back, he said. I stayed on another month, looked after his employees, who were working in his office under the supervision of tax officials, kept the house clean and the garden tidy, and took care of the laundry. I used to take clean laundry to Mr Fehnern in the detention jail, and food too, especially Ardennes pâté, which I had learned how to make at the Gerbers butcher shop in Kuir. Later on the office was closed, the house confiscated, and I had to give up my room. Apparently they had found evidence of embezzlement and forgery against Mr Fehnern, and he was sent to a regular prison, where I continued to visit him. I also wanted to give him back the two months' salary, but he simply would not hear of it. Very soon I found a position with Dr and Mrs Blorna, whom I had met through Mr Fehnern.

The Blornas live in a house in the new 'South Side' development. Although they offered me a room there, I declined. I longed to be independent at last and to pursue my career more on my own. Dr and Mrs Blorna were very gracious to me. Mrs Blorna – she is a member of a large architectural firm – helped me buy my own apartment in the suburb to the south that was advertised as 'Elegant Riverside Residences'. In their respective capacities of corporation lawyer and architect, Dr and Mrs Blorna were familiar with the project. With Dr Blorna I calculated the financing, interest, and amortization for a two-room apartment with kitchen and bath on the eighth floor, and since by then I had been able to save 7,000 marks and Dr and Mrs Blorna guaranteed my bank loan of 30,000 marks, I was soon able to move into my apartment, early in 1970. At first my minimum monthly payment amounted to about 1,100 marks, but since Dr and Mrs Blorna deducted nothing for my board, and Mrs Blorna even gave me something to take home every night in the way of food and drink, I could live very economically and was able to amortize my loan more quickly than had first been calculated.

For four years I have been in sole charge of the Blorna household. My working hours are from seven in the morning till about four-thirty in the afternoon, when I have finished the housecleaning and shopping and completed preparations for the evening meal. I also take care of all the laundry. Between four-thirty and five-thirty I look after my own apartment and after that usually work another hour and a half to two hours for the elderly Hiepertz couple. In both homes I am paid extra for work on Saturdays and Sundays. In my free time I sometimes work for Kloft's the caterers, or I help out at receptions, parties, weddings, dances, and so on, usually on my own for a fixed fee but sometimes commissioned by Kloft's. My work there consists of job-pricing and general organization, but sometimes I do duty as cook or waitress. My gross income averages 1,800 to 2,300 marks a month. In the eyes of the income-tax department I am self-employed. I pay my taxes and insurance myself. All these things – tax returns, etc. – are looked after free of charge by Dr Blorna's office. Since the spring of 1972 I have owned a 1968 Volkswagen which Werner Klormer, a chef employed at Kloft's, let me have at a good price. It was getting too difficult for me to reach my various places of work by public transportation. With my car I became sufficiently mobile to work at receptions and parties held in hotels farther away.

16

It took from 11.00 a.m. to 12.30 p.m. and, following a one-hour break, from 1.30 to 5.45 p.m. to conclude this part of the interrogation. During the lunch break Katharina Blum refused to accept coffee and a cheese sandwich from the police, nor did earnest and kindly attempts on the part of Policewoman Pletzer and Moeding, Beizmenne's assistant, succeed in altering her attitude. It was clearly impossible for her – as Hach told it – to distinguish between official and personal relations, to understand the necessity for the interrogation. When Beizmenne, who was enjoying his coffee and sandwiches and, collar unbuttoned and tie loosened, not only looked paternal but began to behave paternally, Katharina Blum insisted on being taken back to her cell. It is a matter of record that the two police officers who had been detailed to guard her urged her to accept coffee and sandwiches, but she obstinately shook her head, remained seated on her bunk, smoked a cigarette and, with wrinkled nose and an unmistakable expression, clearly conveyed her disgust at the vomit-spattered toilet in the cell. Later, at the urgings of the policewoman and the two young policemen, she permitted the former to take her pulse, and when this proved to be normal she condescended to have a slice of cake and a cup of tea brought from a nearby café, insisting, however, on paying for them out of her own pocket, although one of the young policemen, the one who had guarded her bathroom door that morning while she was dressing, was prepared to 'treat' her. The opinion of the two policemen and Mrs Pletzer on this episode with Katharina Blum: no sense of humour.

17

The recording of the witness's personal background was resumed at 1.30 p.m. and continued until 5.45 p.m. Beizmenne would have been glad to curtail it, but Blum insisted on every detail, and consent to this was given by the two public prosecutors. Eventually Beizmenne also agreed to this procedure – at first reluctantly, later (astutely enough) on account of disclosures relating to the background, which in his eyes was becoming important.

At about 5.45 p.m. the question of continuing or suspending the interrogation was raised, of whether Blum should be released or escorted to a cell. At about 5.00 p.m. she had actually been induced to accept another pot of tea and a sandwich (ham); furthermore, she consented to carry on with the interrogation, Beizmenne having promised to release her when it was over.

The next subject was her relationship with Else Woltersheim. She was her godmother, said Katharina Blum, she had always taken an interest in her, she was a distant cousin of her mother's; Miss Woltersheim had got in touch with her as soon as she moved to town.

'I was invited to this private dance on 20 February. It was supposed to take place on the 21st, the beginning of Carnival, but the date was put forward because Miss Woltersheim had some professional commitments for that date. It was the first time I had danced in four years. I wish to correct that statement: on various occasions, perhaps, two, three or possibly four times, I had danced at the Blornas after helping out at their parties. At the end of the evening, when I had finished tidying up and doing the dishes, when the coffee was served and Dr Blorna had taken over the bar, they would call me in and I would dance in the living room with Dr Blorna and other guests, gentlemen with university, business, or political connections. After a while I was not all that keen to go along with this idea, and finally I stopped altogether: often the men had had too much to drink and made advances to me. To be more precise: ever since I've had my own car I have declined to join in the dancing. Before that I had to rely on one of the gentlemen taking me home. Sometimes I danced with that gentleman' – she pointed to Hach, who actually blushed – 'over there.' She was not asked whether Hach had been among those who made advances to her.

18

The prolonged nature of the interrogation was explained by the fact that Katharina Blum was remarkably meticulous in checking the entire wording and in having every sentence read aloud to her as it was committed to the record. For example, the advances mentioned in the foregoing paragraph were first recorded as 'amorous', the original wording being that 'the gentlemen became amorous', which Katharina Blum indignantly rejected. A regular argument as to definition ensued between her and the public prosecutors, and between her and Beizmenne, with Katharina asserting that 'becoming amorous' implied reciprocity whereas 'advances' were a one-sided affair, which they had invariably been. Upon her questioners observing that surely this wasn't that important and it would be her fault if the interrogation lasted longer than usual, she said she would not sign any deposition containing the word 'amorous' instead of 'advances'. For her the difference was of crucial significance, and one of the reasons why she had separated from her husband was that he had never been amorous but had consistently made advances.

Similar arguments ensued over the word 'gracious', as applied to the Blornas. The record contained the word 'nice to me', Blum insisted on the word 'gracious', and when the word 'kind' was suggested instead, 'gracious' being considered somewhat old-fashioned, she became indignant and declared that 'niceness' and 'kindness' had nothing to do with 'graciousness'. and it was with graciousness that she felt the Blornas had always treated her.

19

Meanwhile the occupants of the building had been questioned; most of them had little or nothing to tell about Katharina Blum. They had occasionally met in the elevator and passed the time of day, they knew that the red Volkswagen belonged to her, some had thought she was a private secretary, others that she was a buyer in a department store; she had always been smartly turned out, pleasant, although a bit on the reserved side. Among the occupants of the five other apartments on the eighth floor, where Katharina lived, there were only two who had more detailed information to give. One was the owner of a hairdressing salon, a Mrs Schmill, the other a retired employee of the electricity works by the name of Ruhwiedel, and the startling thing was that both statements included the assertion that from time to time Katharina had received or brought home a gentleman visitor. Mrs Schmill maintained that this visitor had come regularly, maybe every two or three weeks, an athletic-looking gentleman of about forty, from an 'obviously superior' background, whereas Mr Ruhwiedel described the visitor as a fairly young fellow who had sometimes entered Miss Blum's apartment alone and sometimes accompanied by Miss Blum. And this, moreover some eight or nine times during the past two years, 'those are only the visits I observed – naturally I can't tell you anything about the ones I did not observe'.

When Katharina was confronted with these statements later that afternoon and required to make response to them, it was Hach who, even before actually putting the question, tried to make things easy for her by suggesting that these visitors might have been the guests who had occasionally driven her home from the Blornas. Katharina, blushing deeply from humiliation and anger, asked tartly whether it was against the law to receive male visitors, and since she refused to make use of the way out he had so kindly prepared for her, or refused to recognize it as such, Hach told her, also a bit tartly, that she must realize that a very serious case was being examined, i.e., the case of Ludwig Götten, a case that had numerous ramifications and had been occupying the police and the public prosecutor's office for more than a year, so now he was going to ask her whether the visits, which she was evidently not denying, had always been from one and the same person. And at this point Beizmenne intervened roughly, saying: 'So you've known Götten for two years!'

Katharina was so taken aback by this remark that she was at a loss for an answer; she merely looked at Beizmenne and shook her head, and the answer she stammered out – a surprisingly mild 'No, no, I met him only yesterday' – did not sound very convincing. Upon now being ordered to identify the visitor she shook her head 'almost in horror' and refused to give any names.

Here Beizmenne resumed his paternal role and tried to persuade her, saying there was nothing wrong in having a boyfriend who – and here he made a crucial psychological error – rather than making advances had perhaps been amorous with her; after all, she was divorced and no longer bound by marriage vows, and it was not even – third crucial error! – reprehensible for amorousness occasionally to result in certain material benefits. And at this Katharina Blum finally dug in her heels. She refused to make any further statement and insisted on being taken either home or to a cell. To the surprise of all those present, Beizmenne, subdued and weary – by this time it was 8.40 p.m. – said he would have her taken home by a police officer. But then, when she had already risen and was gathering up her handbag, toilet articles, and the plastic bag, he suddenly barked the question at her: 'How in the world did that amorous Ludwig of yours get out of the building last night? Every entrance, every exit, was guarded – *you* must have known a way and shown it to him, and I'm going to get to the bottom of it. Good night!'

20

Moeding, Beizmenne's assistant, who drove Katharina home, later reported that he was very concerned about the young woman's condition and feared she might resort to something desperate: she was absolutely shattered, done for, and oddly enough it was only in this state that she had revealed, or maybe developed, a sense of humour. Driving through town with her, he said, he had jokingly asked her whether it wouldn't have been nice to go somewhere where they could have had a drink and dance, with no embarrassment, no ulterior motive, and she had nodded and said that wouldn't be bad at all, might even be nice, and then, when they stopped outside her building and he offered to take her up to her apartment, she had said, sarcastically: 'Hm, better not, I have enough gentlemen visitors, as you know – but thanks just the same.'

Throughout the evening and half the night Moeding tried to convince Beizmenne that Katharina Blum should be taken into custody for her own protection, and when Beizmenne asked him whether he might be in love he said, No, he just liked her, and she was his own age, and he didn't believe in Beizmenne's theory of a major conspiracy in which Katharina was involved.

What he did not report, but Blorna was informed of by Miss Woltersheim, was the two pieces of advice Moeding gave Katharina, who did not object to his accompanying her through the lobby as far as the elevator: somewhat risky advice that might have cost him dearly and, moreover, endangered the lives of himself and his colleagues, for what he said to Katharina as they stood by the elevator was: 'Don't touch the phone, and don't look at the news tomorrow', from which it was not clear whether he meant the *News* or simply the news.

21

It was at about 3.30 on the afternoon of the same day (Thursday, 21 February 1974) that Blorna was for the first time putting on his skis at his winter resort in preparation for a cross-country run. From this moment on the vacation to which he had been looking forward for so many weeks was ruined. How glorious the walk had been last evening, shortly after their arrival, tramping for two hours through the snow with Trude, then the bottle of wine by the fireside and the deep sleep beside the open window: lingering over their first breakfast, and again lounging on the terrace for a few hours, warmly wrapped up, and just then, at the very moment when he was planning to set out, this fellow from the *News* had turned up and, with no preamble, started quizzing him about Katharina. Did Blorna consider her capable of committing a crime? 'What do you mean?' he replied, 'I'm an attorney and I know that all kinds of people are capable of committing a crime. What crime are you talking about. Katharina? Out of the question, what in the world gave you that idea? What makes you think such a thing?'

On finally being told that a wanted man was known to have spent the night in Katharina's apartment and that since about eleven that morning she had been the object of intensive questioning, his first thought was to fly home and be by her side, but the fellow from the *News* – did he really look that unsavoury, or did Blorna get that impression later? – said, Well, things weren't really as bad as all that and couldn't Dr Blorna tell him a bit about her character? And when he refused, the fellow told him that was a bad sign and could be misconstrued, for to refuse to comment on her character in a case of this kind – and this was a front-page story – was a clear implication of a bad character, and Blorna, by now furious and irritated in the extreme, said: 'Katharina is a very intelligent, cool, level-headed person', and was annoyed because that wasn't true either and nowhere near conveying what he had wanted to say and ought to have said. He had never had anything to do with newspapers, let alone the *News*, and when the fellow drove off again in his Porsche Blorna unfastened his skis and knew he could forget about his vacation. He went upstairs and found Trude lying on the balcony, snugly tucked up and dozing in the sun. He told her what had happened. 'Why don't you call her?' she said, and he made three, four, five attempts to reach her by telephone, but each time the operator's voice came back saying 'Your party does not answer'. He tried again around eleven that night, but again there was no answer. He drank a lot and slept badly.

22

On Friday morning when he appeared for breakfast around 9.30 looking thoroughly out of sorts, Trude held out the *News* to him. Katharina on the front page. Huge photo, huge type.

KATHARINA BLUM,
OUTLAW'S SWEETHEART,
REFUSES INFORMATION
ON MALE VISITORS

Ludwig Götten, the outlaw and murderer who has been

sought by the police for a year and a half, could have been arrested yesterday if his mistress, Katharina Blum, a domestic, had not destroyed all traces of him and covered his escape. It is assumed by the police that the Blum woman has been involved in the conspiracy for some time. (For further details see back page: MALE VISITORS.)

On the back page he saw that the *News* had transformed his statement that Katharina was intelligent, cool, and level-headed into 'ice-cold and calculating', and his general observations on crime now read that she was 'entirely capable of committing a crime'.

The pastor of Gemmelsbroich had the following to say: 'I wouldn't put anything past her. Her father was a Communist in disguise, and her mother, whom on compassionate grounds I employed for a time as a charwoman, stole the sacramental wine and carried on orgies in the sacristy with her lovers.'

For the last two years the Blum woman has regularly received male visitors. Was her apartment a conspiracy hangout, a gang's headquarters, an arms cache? How did the 27-year-old domestic come by an apartment worth an estimated 110,000 marks? Did she share in the loot from the bank holdups? The police are pursuing their inquiries. The office of the public prosecutor is working around the clock. More details tomorrow. THE *News* IS ALWAYS WHERE THE ACTION IS! *Complete story in tomorrow's weekend edition.*

That afternoon, at the airport, Blorna reconstructed the swift sequence of events that followed:

10.25: Phone call from Lüding, very worked up, urging me to return at once and get in touch with Alois, who was equally worked up. Alois, described by Lüding as quite beside himself – since I have never seen him like that I consider it unlikely – at present attending a conference of Christian businessmen at Bad Bedelig where he is the main speaker and has to lead the discussion.

10.40: Call from Katharina asking me whether I had really said what was in the *News*. Glad to be able to set her right and explain what had happened, and she said (as far as I remember) something like: 'I believe you, I really do, I know now the way these bastards work. This morning they even ferreted out my mother, who is a very sick woman, as well as Brettloh and some other people.' On my asking her where she was she said: 'At Else's, and now I have to go back for more questioning.'

11.00: Call from Alois, whom for the first time in my life – and I've known him for twenty years – I heard in a state of agitation and alarm. Told me I must return at once to represent him in a very delicate matter, he had to give his paper now, then have lunch with the businessmen, after that lead the discussion, and in the evening attend an informal get-together, but he could be at our place some time between 7.30 and 9.30 and would still have time to drop in at the informal get-together.

11.30: Trude also feels we should leave immediately and stand by Katharina. I can tell from her ironical smile that she already has a theory (probably correct, as always) as to Alois's problems.

12.15: Reservations made, packing done, bill paid. After a vacation lasting barely forty hours, in taxi en route to I. At the airport in I., waited from 2 to 3 p.m. for fog to lift. Long talk with Trude about Katharina, of whom, as Trude knows, I am very, very fond. Also discussed how we had encouraged Katharina not to be so supersensitive but to forget her unhappy childhood and unfortunate marriage. How we had tried to overcome her pride in money matters and to arrange for cheaper credit from our own funds than she could get from the bank. Even when we explained that, if she gave us 9 per cent instead of the 14 per cent she has to pay the bank, we would lose nothing and she would save quite a bit, she was not convinced. How much we owe Katharina! Since she has been running our home in her quiet, pleasant manner, not only have our expenses gone down but the extent to which she has freed us for our professional lives is almost impossible to express in terms of money. She has released us from the chaos that for five years had been weighing so heavily on our marriage and our professional lives.

Decide about 4.30 that the fog doesn't look as if it's going to lift and so to take the train. On Trude's advice I do *not* call Alois Sträubleder. Taxi to station, where we just manage to catch the 5.45 for Frankfurt. Wretched journey – nausea, frayed nerves. Even Trude serious and worried. She has a sense of foreboding. In spite of utter exhaustion changed trains in Munich, managed to get a sleeper. We both anticipate trouble with and over Katharina, problems with Lüding and Sträubleder.

23

Right on Saturday morning, on arriving at the station in the still celebrating city, rumpled and wretched as the couple was: right there on the platform is the *News*, once again with Katharina on the front page, now shown walking down the steps of police headquarters accompanied by a plainclothes police officer. MURDERER'S MOLL WON'T TALK! NO HINT AS TO GÖTTEN'S WHEREABOUTS! POLICE ON FULL ALERT.

Trude bought the rag, and in silence they took a cab. As he was paying the driver while Trude was opening the front door, the driver pointed to the *News*, saying: 'You're in there too, I recognized you right off. You're that broad's attorney, and her boss too, right?' Blorna overtipped the man who, with a grin that seemed less gloating than his tone of voice, carried their bags and skis into the hall and gave them a pleasant 'So long now'.

Trude had already plugged in the coffee-maker and was washing her hands in the bathroom. The *News* lay on the table in the living room together with two telegrams, one from Lüding and the other from Sträubleder. Lüding's: 'Your failure to contact me disappointing to say the least. Lüding.' Sträubleder's: 'Fail to understand your letting me down like this. Expect immediate call. Alois.'

It was just on eight-fifteen, almost the very hour at which Katharina normally served their breakfast: how attractively she always set the table, with flowers, freshly laundered tablecloth and napkins, various kinds of bread, honey, eggs, and coffee, and, for Trude, toast and marmalade.

Even Trude waxed almost sentimental as she brought in the coffee, a few slices of rye crisp, some butter and honey. 'It'll never be the same, never. They'll destroy that girl. If not the police, then the *News*, and when the *News* has finished with her it'll be the public. Here, read this first, then phone those gentlemen visitors.' He read:

The *News*, in its unceasing efforts to keep its readers fully abreast of events, has been successful in gathering further information throwing light on the character of Blum and her murky past. *News* reporters managed to ascertain the whereabouts of Miss Blum's invalid mother, who began by complaining that her daughter had not been to see her for a long time. Then, when confronted by the irrefutable facts, she said: 'It was bound to come to this, it was bound to end like this.' Miss Blum's former husband, Wilhelm Brettloh, a respectable textile worker who divorced his wife on grounds of wilful desertion, was even more eager to supply the *News* with information: 'Now,' he said, barely managing to restrain his

35

tears, 'now I know why she walked out on me. Why she threw me over. *That's* what was going on. I see it all now. Our modest happiness was not enough for her. She was ambitious, and how is an honest, modest workingman ever to come by a Porsche? Maybe' (he added sagely) 'you can pass my advice along to your readers: That's how false ideas about socialism are bound to end. ask you and your readers: How does a housemaid come by such wealth? Not honestly, that's for sure. Now I know why I was always scared by her radical views, her hostility to the Church, and I bless Our Lord's wisdom in not sending us children. Now when I learn that she prefers the caresses of a murderer and a thief to my straightforward affection, that part is explained too. And yet I feel bound to cry out to her: My little Katharina, if only you had stayed with me! As the years went by we too would one day have been able to own a home and a small car. I could hardly have offered you a Porsche, merely such modest happiness as can be offered by an honest workingman who doesn't trust the unions. Ah, Katharina!'

Also on the back page, under the heading 'RETIRED COUPLE HORRIFIED BUT NOT SURPRISED', Blorna found a column marked in red:

Berthold Hiepertz, retired high-school principal, and his wife Mrs Erna Hiepertz, appeared horrified to learn of Blum's activities but not 'especially surprised'. In Lemgo a woman reporter from the *News* called on the couple at the home of their married daughter, director of a sanatorium in that town, and Mr Hiepertz, teacher of classical languages and history in whose home Blum had worked for three years, stated: 'In every respect a very radical person who cleverly succeeded in deceiving us.'

(Hiepertz, whom Blorna telephoned later, swore that what he had actually said was: 'If Katharina is a radical, then she is radical in her helpfulness, her organizing ability, and her intelligence – or I am very much mistaken in her, and I have had forty years' experience as a teacher and have seldom been deceived.')

(Continued from page 1:)

Miss Blum's former husband, now a competely broken man, on whom the *News* called during a rehearsal by the Gemmelsbroich Fife & Drum Corps, turned aside to conceal his tears. The other corps members, to quote Mr Meffels, retired farmer, also turned aside in horror from Katharina, who had always acted so strangely and always pretended to be so easily shocked. The innocent Carnival pleasures of an honest workingman might well be said to have been clouded.

And finally a picture of Blorna and Trude, in their garden beside the swimming pool. Caption: 'What is the role of Mrs Blorna, once known as "Trude the Red", and her husband, who sometimes describes himself as "Leftist"? Dr Blorna, highly paid corporation lawyer, with his wife Trude beside the swimming pool at their luxury home.'

24

This is the moment for a kind of backing-up process for what is known in movies and literature as a flashback: from the Saturday morning when Dr and Mrs Blorna, travel-worn and somewhat desperate, returned from their vacation, to the Friday morning when Katharina was once again taken to police headquarters for questioning, this time by Policewoman Pletzer and an older police officer who was only lightly armed, and she was picked up not from her own apartment but from Miss Woltersheim's, to which Katharina had driven around five o'clock that morning, this time in her car. The policewoman made no bones about knowing she would find Katharina at Miss Wolters-heim's rather than at her own home. (In all justice we must not fail to recall the sacrifices and ordeals endured by Dr and Mrs Blorna: breaking off of their vacation, cab drive to the airport near I. Waiting in the fog. Cab to railway station. Catching the Frankfurt train plus changing at Munich. Being rattled about in the sleeper and, early in the morning, having hardly arrived home, already confronted by the *News*! Later – too late, of course – Blorna regretted that, instead of trying to telephone Katharina, who he knew was being questioned, he had not called Hach.)

What struck all those participating in Katharina's second interrogation on Friday – once again Moeding, Police-woman Pletzer, Public Prosecutors Korten and Hach, and Anna Lockster, stenographer (who was irritated by Blum's linguistic sensitivity and called her 'stuck-up') – what struck all of these people was Beizmenne's mood of high good humour. He entered the room rubbing his hands, treated Katharina with great consideration, apologized for 'certain incivilities' that stemmed from his own personality rather than his office, it was just that he was rather a rough dia-mond, and then started by picking up the itemized list that had been drawn up of all the confiscated articles. These were as follows:

1. One small, well-worn green notebook, containing no-thing but telephone numbers; these had meanwhile been checked out and revealed nothing of a compromising nature. Katharina Blum had evidently been using this notebook for almost ten years. A handwriting expert who had been trying to trace Götten by his handwriting (Götten had been, among other things, an army deserter and had worked in an office, thus leaving a number of handwriting traces) had described the development of Katharina's handwriting as a classic example: the girl who at sixteen had made a note of the

telephone number of Gerbers the butcher, at seventeen the number of Dr Kluthen, physician, at twenty while working for Mr Fehnern – and later – the numbers and addresses of caterers, restaurateurs, and those working in her own line of business.

2. Bank statements in which every transaction in her savings account had been meticulously identified by her own handwritten marginal notes. Each sum credited or debited to the account – all correct and not one of them suspicious. The same applied to her entries and notes, contained in a small file, on the state of her commitments to the Haftex company, from which she had bought her apartment at 'Elegant Riverside Residences'. In addition her tax declarations, assessments, and payments had been thoroughly examined and checked out by an accountant, and nowhere could that expert discover any 'substantial concealed amount'. Beizmenne had considered it important to examine her financial transactions especially over the two preceding years, which he facetiously referred to as the 'male visitor period'. Nothing. However, it transpired that Katharina remitted 150 marks to her mother every month, and that she had a standing order with the firm of Kolter in Kuir for the care of her father's grave in Gemmelsbroich. The furniture she had bought, her household utensils, clothes, underwear, gasoline bills – all checked out and nowhere a discrepancy. In handing back the files to Beizmenne, the accountant remarked: 'All I can say is, if she's released and is ever looking for a job – tip me off, will you? This is what we're always looking for and can never find.' Nor did the Blum telephone bills yield any grounds for suspicion. It was apparent from them that she almost never made long-distance calls.

Further it was noted that now and again Katharina Blum had remitted small sums of 15 to 30 marks to her brother

Kurt, then serving a sentence for breaking and entering, to augment his pocket money. Blum paid no church taxes. As shown by her financial records, she had left the Catholic Church at the age of nineteen in 1966.

3. A second small notebook with various entries, mainly figures, contained four columns: one for the Blorna household with amounts for grocery shopping and expenditures on cleaning materials, dry cleaning, laundry. From these entries it was clear that Katharina did all the ironing herself. The second column was for the Hiepertz home with similar details and accounts. A third was for her own home, which she evidently ran on a very modest budget; there were months when she had spent scarcely 30 to 50 marks on food. However, she did seem to go quite often to the movies – she had no television set – and occasionally to buy herself chocolate bars and even a box of chocolates.

The fourth column itemized income and expenditure in connection with the extra jobs she took on and involved the purchase and laundering of uniforms as well as a proportion of the running expenses for her Volkswagen. At this point – the figures for gasoline – Beizmenne interrupted with an amiability that surprised everyone and asked her to account for the relatively high figures for gasoline, figures which, incidentally, tallied with the noticeably high figure on her odometer. It had been ascertained, he said, that the distance to the Blornas and back was about 6 kilometres, to the Hiepertzes and back about 8, to Miss Woltersheim's about 4, and if one were to reckon an average of one extra job a week (a generous estimate) and allow 20 kilometres for that (which was also generous and amounted to about 3 kilometres for each weekday) one would arrive at roughly 21 to 22 kilometres per day. And it must be considered that she did not visit Miss Woltersheim every day, but never mind about that. In other words, one arrived at some 8,000 kilometres a year, whereas when she – Katharina Blum – had acquired the VW six years ago the written agreement with Klormer the chef showed that at that time the car had had 56,000 kilometres on it. If one were to add six times 8,000 to that figure, her odometer should now show somewhere in the neighbourhood of 104,000 to 105,000, whereas the actual figure was 162,000. Now it was known that from time to time she went to visit her mother in Gemmelsbroich and later at the sanatorium in Kuir-Hochsackel, and no doubt also her brother in jail – but the distance to Gemmelsbroich or Kuir-Hochsackel was about 50 kilometres there and back and to her brother about 60, and if one were to reckon one, or, to be generous, two visits a month (and her brother had been in jail only for the last year and a half, before that he had lived with their mother in Gemmelsbroich), well then – still calculating on the basis of six years – one would arrive at a further 7,000 to 8,000 kilometres, and there still remained a figure of between 45,000 and 50,000 unexplained, i.e., unaccounted for. So where had she driven to so often? Had she – he really didn't want to offer crude suggestions again, but she must understand his question – had she perhaps been meeting one or more persons somewhere – and, if so, where?

Fascinated, also shocked, not only Katharina Blum but all those present listened to Beizmenne's calculation presented in a mild voice, and it seemed as if Katharina, while Beizmenne was presenting these figures to her, did not even feel angry, merely a tension made up of shock and fascination, because, as he was speaking, she was not searching for an explanation of the 50,000 kilometres: she was trying to figure out where and when she had driven why and where to. On sitting down at the start of the interrogation she had been surprisingly approachable, almost 'relaxed', she had even seemed a bit nervous and had accepted some tea without even insisting on paying for it herself. And now, when Beizmenne had finished with his questions and calculations, a deathly silence – to quote many, *almost* all, of those present – reigned, as if there were a feeling that someone, on the basis of a discovery which (had it not been for the gasoline bills) might easily have been overlooked, had now actually penetrated an intimate secret of Katharina Blum, whose life up to that moment had appeared to be an open book.

Yes [said Katharina Blum, and from now on her statement was recorded and exists in the transcript] that's right, that amounts to – I've just worked it out quickly in my head – almost 25 kilometres a day. I never gave a thought to it, nor to the cost either, but sometimes I would just drive off, simply get in the car and drive, with no destination in mind – or rather, somehow there always did turn out to be a destination, I mean I would drive in a direction that just seemed to suggest itself, south towards Coblenz, or west towards Aachen, or down to the Lower Rhine. Not every day. I can't say how often or at what intervals. Usually when it was raining and I had finished work and was by myself. No, I wish to correct that statement: it was *only* when it was raining that I went for drives like that. I don't know why exactly. You must remember that sometimes, when I didn't have to go to the Hiepertzes and had no extra job lined up, I would be home by five o'clock with nothing to do. I didn't always want to go and see Else, especially since she's become so friendly with Konrad, and to go to the movies alone isn't always all that safe for a woman on her own. Sometimes I would go and sit in a church, not for religious reasons but because you can be quiet there, but these days you find people buttonholing you in churches too, and they're not always laymen either. I do have a few friends, of course: Werner Klormer, for instance, from whom I bought my Volkswagen, and his wife, and some of the other staff at Kloft's, but it is rather difficult, and usually embarrassing, to turn up alone without automatically, or I should say, unconditionally, falling in with every suggestion that offers. And so then I would just get into the car, turn on the radio, and drive off, always on secondary roads, always in the rain, and the roads I liked best were the ones with trees – sometimes I got as far as Holland or Belgium, would have a cup of coffee or a beer there, and drive home again. Yes. Now that you ask me I see it all. So – if you ask me how often, I would say: two or three times a month – sometimes less, sometimes maybe more often, and usually for several hours, until at about nine or ten, sometimes not till eleven, I would come home, dead tired. It may have been partly fear too: I know too many lonely women who spend their evenings getting drunk in front of the TV.

The gentle smile with which Beizmenne absorbed this explanation, without comment, gave no hint as to what was going on in his mind. He merely nodded, and if he rubbed his hands again it must have been because Katharina Blum's information had confirmed one of his theories. For a while everything was very quiet, as if those present were surprised or embarrassed; it seemed as if for the first time Blum had revealed something personal and intimate. After that the itemization of the remaining confiscated articles was swiftly disposed of.

4. One photograph album containing snapshots of persons who were all easily identified. Katharina Blum's father, who looked ailing and bitter and far older than he could have been. Her mother who, it was disclosed, was dying of cancer. Her brother. Katharina herself, at four, at six, as a First Communicant at ten, as a bride of twenty; her husband; the Gemmelsbroich pastor, neighbours, relatives, various photos of Else Woltersheim; then an older man, not immediately identifiable, who looked rather jolly and turned out to be Mr Fehnern, the guilty accountant. Not a single picture of anyone who could be made to link up with Beizmenne's theories.

5. A passport issued in the name of Katharina Brettloh née Blum. In connection with this item, she was asked questions about travel, and it turned out that she had never 'been on a real trip' and, except for a few days when she had been off sick, had always worked. She had received her vacation pay from the Fehnerns and the Blornas, but she had either gone on working or taken extra jobs.

6. One old chocolate box. Contents: some letters, scarcely a dozen, from her mother, brother, husband, Miss Woltersheim. None containing the slightest indication that bore on the suspicion resting upon her. The box also contained a few loose snapshots of her father as a private in the German Army and of her husband in the uniform of the Fife & Drum Corps, a few torn-off calendar pages with mottoes, and a sizeable handwritten collection of her own recipes plus a pamphlet entitled 'The Use of Sherry in Sauces'.

7. One binder containing certificates, diplomas, and records, all her divorce papers, and the certified documents relating to her condominium apartment.

8. Three bunches of keys. These had been checked out and found to be house and closet keys to her own apartment, the Blornas' home, and the Hiepertzes'.

It was established and recorded that no suspicious clue had been found among the above-mentioned articles; Katharina Blum's explanation of her gas consumption and the kilometres she had driven was accepted without comment.

Only now did Beizmenne draw from his pocket a ruby ring, set with diamonds, that he had apparently been keeping there loose, for he polished it on his jacket sleeve before holding it out to Katharina.

'Do you recognize this ring?'

'Yes,' she said, without hesitation or embarrassment.

'Does it belong to you?'

'Yes.'

'Do you know what it is worth?'

'Not exactly. It can't be much.'

'Well now,' said Beizmenne pleasantly, 'we have had it appraised, and as a precautionary measure not only by our expert here in the building but also, so as to be sure and not do you an injustice, by a local jeweller. This ring is worth between eight and ten thousand marks. You didn't know that? I am prepared to believe you, but I must still ask you to explain where you got it. In the context of an inquiry concerning a criminal convicted of robbery and strongly suspected of murder, a ring of this kind is no trivial matter, nor is it a private and personal matter such as a few hundred kilometres or driving around for hours in the rain. Now from whom did you receive this ring? From Götten or the gentleman visitor, or perhaps Götten *was* the gentleman visitor? And if not: where did you drive to as a "lady visitor", if I may use the term facetiously – in the rain for thousands of kilometres? It would be a simple matter for us to find out from which jeweller the ring was obtained, and whether it was bought or stolen, but I would like to give you a chance – I do not, you see, consider you directly involved in a criminal capacity, merely naive and a little too romantic. How do you propose to explain to me – to us – that you, a person known to be easily shocked, almost prudish, a person whose friends have nicknamed "the nun", who avoids discotheques because of the depraved goings-on there, who gets a divorce because her husband "made advances" to her – how do you propose to explain that you (so you say) did not meet this man Götten until the day before yesterday and yet that very day – one might say, post haste – took him home and there very rapidly became, well, shall we say, intimate with him? What do you call that? Love at first sight? Infatuation? Amorous feelings? Don't you see that there are certain inconsistencies there which do not altogether preclude suspicion? And there is something else.' He put his hand in his jacket pocket and drew out a rather large white envelope from which he extracted a somewhat fancy, mauve, cream-lined envelope of normal dimensions. 'This empty envelope which, together with the ring, we found in your night-table drawer, is postmarked 12 February 1974, 6.00 p.m., Düsseldorf Station Post Office – and addressed to you. For Heaven's sake,' Biezmenne said in conclusion, 'if you have had a boyfriend who visited you from time to time and whom you sometimes drove to see, who wrote you letters and sometimes gave you presents – go ahead and tell us, it's not a crime! It would only incriminate you if there were some connection with Götten.'

It was clear to everyone in the room that Katharina recognized the ring but had not known its value; that here again the sensitive subject of male visitors was being raised. Was she ashamed because she saw a threat to her reputation, or did she see a threat to someone else whom she did not want to implicate in the affair? This time she only blushed slightly. Would she not admit to having received the ring from Götten because she knew it would not have been very convincing to try and present Götten as that kind of cavalier? She remained calm, 'subdued' almost, as she testified:

'It is true that at Miss Woltersheim's party I danced exclusively and fervently with Ludwig Götten, whom I saw for the first time in my life and whose surname I did not discover until I was being questioned by the police on Thursday morning. I felt a great tenderness for him and he for me. I left Miss Woltersheim's apartment around ten o'clock and drove with Ludwig Götten to my apartment.

'As to the origin of the ring I cannot – correction: I do not wish to – give any information. Since it did not come into my possession in any irregular manner, I do not feel

46

obliged to account for its origin. The sender of the envelope produced for my inspection is unknown to me. I take it to be one of the usual specimens of advertising material. I am by this time quite well known in the catering business. Why an advertisement should be sent to me with no sender's name in a fancy lined envelope is something I cannot explain. I would merely like to point out that some firms in the food business are anxious to project a glamorous image.'

On then being asked why on that particular day, although she was obviously – and by her own admission – so fond of driving, why on that particular day she had taken the street-car to Miss Woltersheim's, Katharina Blum said she had not known whether she would have a lot to drink or a little, and it had seemed safer not to take her own car. When asked whether she drank a lot or even sometimes became intoxicated, she said, No, she did not drink much and she had never been intoxicated, and only once – and that had been in the presence and at the instigation of her husband at a social evening of the Fife & Drum Corps – had she been *made* intoxicated, and that had been with some aniseed stuff that tasted like lemonade. Later she had been told that this somewhat expensive stuff was very popular for getting people drunk. When it was pointed out to her that this explanation – of having feared she might have too much to drink – did not hold water since she never drank much, and did she not realize that it must look as if she had had a regular assignation with Götten and so had known she would not need her car but would drive home in his, she shook her head, saying it was exactly as she had stated. She had certainly felt in the mood for drinking a bit more than usual, but in the end she had not done so.

One further point remained to be clarified before the lunch break: Why had she no savings book or cheque book? Maybe she did have a cheque account somewhere after all?

No, the only account she had was the one at the savings bank. Every sum at her disposal, even the smallest, she immediately applied to her loan, on which the interest was so high; sometimes this interest amounted to almost double the interest on her savings, and on a cheque account there was hardly any interest at all. Besides, she found it too expensive and too complicated to use cheques. All her running expenses, for her home and for her car, she paid in cash.

25

Certain blockages, also definable as tensions or pressures, are, of course, unavoidable inasmuch as not all sources can be diverted and/or rerouted at one go and all at once, so that dry land is immediately exposed. However, unnecessary tensions are to be avoided, and we will now try to explain why on this Friday morning not only Beizmenne but also Katharina behaved in such a mild, not to say subdued manner, Katharina seeming even nervous or intimidated. While it was true that the *News*, which a friendly neighbour had pushed under Miss Woltersheim's front door, had aroused anger, exasperation, indignation, shame, and fear in both women, the immediately ensuing telephone conversation with Blorna had mitigated these emotions; and since, shortly after the two horrified women had skimmed through the *News* and Katharina had telephoned Blorna, Policewoman Pletzer had arrived and frankly admitted that naturally Katharina's apartment was being kept under surveillance and that was how she knew she would find Katharina here, and now unfortunately they had to go – Miss Woltersheim too, unfortunately – to police headquarters for questioning, the shock caused by the *News* gave way temporarily before

Policewoman Pletzer's candid, pleasant manner, and Katharina was once again able to dwell on something that had occurred during the night and that had made her very happy: Ludwig had called her, and from *there*!

He had been so sweet, and that was why she had told him nothing of all this trouble because she didn't want him to feel he was the cause of any unhappiness. Nor did they mention love, she had expressly forbidden him to do that even on the way home with him in the car. No, no, she was fine, of course she would rather be with him and stay with him for ever or at least for a long time, preferably for ever and ever, of course, and she would rest up during Carnival and never, never again dance with any other man but him, and never anything but Latin American, and only with him, and what were things like where he was? The accommodation was fine, and he had everything he needed, and since she had forbidden him to mention love all he wanted to say was that he liked her very, very, very much, and one day – he didn't yet know when, it might be months or even a couple of years – he would come for her and take her away, he didn't yet know where to. And so on, the way people do chat on the phone when they feel a great affection for one another. No mention of intimacies, let alone any word about that event which Beizmenne (or, as becomes increasingly likely: Hach) had so crudely specified. And so on. Merely the things this kind of tender loving couple finds to say to each other. For quite some time. Ten minutes. Maybe even more, Katharina told Else. Perhaps, as far as the actual vocabulary of the two young lovers is concerned, one may also refer to certain modern movies in which a good deal of chitchat plus a good deal of *seemingly* inconsequential chitchat goes on in telephone conversations – often over great distances.

The telephone conversation between Katharina and Ludwig had, moreover, been the cause of Beizmenne's relaxed and pleasant mood of leniency; and although he thought he knew why Katharina had dropped all that stubborn stand-offish attitude, she, of course, could not suspect that his cheerful mood stemmed from the same event, although not for the same reason. (This notable and noteworthy process should prompt us to telephone more often – even, if need be, without tender whisperings – since we can never know *who* may derive pleasure from such a call.) But Beizmenne knew the reason for Katharina's nervousness, for he was also aware of a further telephone call, an anonymous one.

The reader is asked not to explore the sources of confidential information contained in this chapter: it is merely that the amateurishly erected earth wall of a subsidiary puddle has been breached and the water drawn off and/or caused to flow out before the weak retaining wall collapses and all that pressure and tension is drained away.

26

To avoid any misunderstanding it must be noted that naturally both Else Woltersheim and Blorna were aware that Katharina had committed an offence by helping Götten to slip out unseen from her apartment; indeed, the fact that she had provided him with an escape route made her an accessory to certain criminal acts, even if in this case not the relevant ones! Else Woltersheim told her this point-blank, shortly before Policewoman Pletzer came to pick them both up for questioning. Blorna seized the first opportunity to draw Katharina's attention to the criminal nature of her action. Nor should Katharina's remark to Miss Woltersheim about Götten be withheld: 'But don't you see – he was simply the One who was to come, and I would have married him and had children with him – even if I had had to wait years till he got out of jail!'

27

The interrogation of Katharina could thus be considered at an end; she had merely to be available for a possible confrontation with statements made by the other Woltersheim guests. For it was now necessary to clarify a question that, in the context of Beizmenne's theory of a prearranged assignation and conspiracy, was sufficiently important: How had Ludwig Götten come to be a guest at the Woltersheim dance?

Katharina Blum was told that she could decide whether to go home or to wait in some place of her choice, but she declined to go home, saying that events had spoiled the apartment for her once and for all, and that she preferred to wait in a cell until Miss Woltersheim had been questioned, and then to go home with her. Only now did Katharina take the two issues of the *News* from her handbag and ask whether the government – as she put it – could not do something to protect her from this filth and to restore her lost honour. She was now well aware that her interrogation was perfectly justified, although she could not quite see the point of this 'going into every last intimate detail', but she could not understand how details arising out of the interrogation – the gentlemen visitors, for instance – could ever have come to the knowledge of the *News*, and all those lying and fraudulent statements. At this point Hach, the public prosecutor, intervened, saying that, in view of the enormous public interest in the Götten case, it had, of course been necessary to issue a statement for the press; as yet there had been no press conference, but owing to the excitement and apprehension generated by Götten's escape – which Katharina must remember she had made feasible – it would hardly be possible to avoid one. Moreover, the mere fact of knowing Götten had made her a 'public figure' and thus the object of justifiable public interest. She was free to bring a private suit on the grounds of insulting and possibly libellous details in the newspaper reports and, if it should turn out that there had been 'leaks' in official circles, she could rest assured that the police authorities would bring charges against a person or persons unknown and support her in the restitution of her rights.

Katharina Blum was then escorted to a cell. It was not considered necessary to put her under strict guard; she was assigned a fairly young woman police assistant, Renate Zündach, who stayed with her, unarmed, and reported later that throughout the whole period – some two and a half hours – Katharina Blum had done nothing but read the two issues of the *News* over and over again. Tea, sandwiches – she refused them all, not aggressively but in 'quite a pleasant, rather apathetic way'. Every attempt to discuss clothes, movies, dancing, which she, Renate Zündach, tried to initiate in order to take Blum's mind off her problems, had been repulsed by Katharina.

Then, Zündach reported, in order to help Blum, who seemed positively hypnotized by the *News*, she had asked her colleague Hüften to relieve her for a few minutes and had gone off to the archives, returning with clippings from other newspapers in which Blum's involvement and interrogation, and her potential role, had been reported quite matter-of-factly. They carried brief accounts on the third or fourth page that did not even give Blum's full name, referring merely to a certain Katharina B., a domestic. In the

Review, for example, there had been a mere ten-line report, with no picture, in which mention was made of the unfortunate involvement of a completely blameless person. All this – she had placed fifteen newspaper clippings in front of Blum, she said – failed to console her: Katharina had merely asked: 'Who reads those anyway? Everyone *I* know reads the *News*!'

28

In order to clarify how Götten came to be at the Woltersheim dance, the first to be questioned was Else Woltersheim herself, and from the outset it became clear that, in her attitude towards the entire body of men by whom she was being questioned, Miss Woltersheim was, if not downright hostile, certainly more hostile than Blum. She stated that she had been born in 1930, was thus forty-four, unmarried, occupation housekeeper-cateress. Before testifying about the affair itself she gave her opinion, in an 'unemotional, dry-as-dust tone of voice, which lent more strength to her indignation than if she had shouted or screamed abuse', on the treatment of Katharina Blum by the *News* as well as on the fact that details from the interrogation were evidently being leaked to that kind of publication. She realized that Katharina's role had to be examined, but she wondered if 'the destruction of a young life', as was now taking place, could be justified. She had known Katharina, she went on, since the day she was born, and could already observe the havoc being wrought in her since yesterday. She was no psychologist, but the fact that Katharina had obviously lost all interest in her apartment, of which she had been so fond and for which she had worked so hard, was, in her opinion, alarming.

It was not easy to interrupt Miss Woltersheim's torrent of complaint, it was too much even for Beizmenne, and only when he broke in to reproach her for admitting Götten into her home did she say that she hadn't even known his name, he hadn't introduced himself nor had anyone introduced him to her. All she knew was that, on the Wednesday in question, at around 7.30 p.m., he had turned up in the company of Hertha Scheumel, who had come with her friend Claudia Sterm, who in turn was in the company of a man dressed as a sheikh of whom all she knew was that they called him Karl and who later in the evening behaved in a distinctly odd manner. There could be no question of any prearranged meeting with this man Götten, nor had she ever heard his name before, and she knew all about Katharina's life down to the last detail. On being confronted with Katharina's statement about her 'mystery drives', she had perforce to admit that she had known nothing about them, and this dealt a crucial blow to her claim to familiarity with every detail of Katharina's life. On the subject of the gentlemen visitors she became embarrassed, saying that, since Katharina had apparently said nothing about them, she also would refuse to comment. The only thing she could say on this subject was: one of them had been a 'rather corny affair', and 'when I say corny I don't mean Katharina, I mean the visitor'. If authorized by Katharina she would tell them all she knew about it; she thought it quite out of the question that Katharina's long drives had taken her to that person. Yes, this man did exist, and if she hesitated to say more about him it was because she did not want him to become a laughing stock. In any case, Katharina's part in both cases – that of Götten and of the gentleman visitor – had been quite beyond reproach. Katharina had always been a hardworking, respectable girl, a bit timid, or rather intimidated, and as a child she had even been a devout and faithful churchgoer.

But then her mother, who used to clean the church in Gemmelsbroich, had been reprimanded several times for irregular behaviour, and once she had even been caught sharing a bottle of sacramental wine with the verger in the sacristy. This had been blown up into an 'orgy' and a scandal, and Katharina had had to suffer in school at the hands of the pastor. Yes, Mrs Blum, Katharina's mother, had been very unstable and at times an alcoholic, but one must picture that husband – Katharina's father – always grumbling, always ailing, who had returned from the war a total wreck, then the embittered mother and the brother, who, one was bound to say, had turned out badly. She also knew the story of the marriage that had gone so hopelessly wrong. In fact, she had advised Katharina against it from the very beginning, Brettloh being an – she apologized for the expression – arse-licker, typical of those who kowtow to all authority, both secular and religious; besides, he was a most disgusting show-off. She had regarded Katharina's early marriage as a flight from her terrible home environment and, as was plain to see, the moment Katharina escaped from that environment and her imprudent marriage, she developed into a wonderful person. Her job qualifications were unimpeachable. That was something to which she – Miss Woltersheim – could attest not only verbally but also, if need be, in writing since she was a member of the Trade Council's examining board. With the growing trend in private and public entertaining towards what was now being called 'organized buffet style', the opportunities for a woman like Katharina Blum were opening out accordingly, since she was a highly suitable person, as well as highly trained in organization, pricing, and attractive presentation. Although now, of course, if she failed to get satisfaction from the *News*, Katharina's interest in her career would fade along with her interest in her apartment.

At this point in her statement, Miss Woltersheim was informed that it was not the job of the police or the public prosecutor's office 'to pursue certain undoubtedly reprehensible forms of journalism by bringing criminal charges'. Freedom of the press was not to be lightly tampered with, and she could rest assured that a private complaint would be handled with justice and a charge on grounds of illegal sources of information brought against a person or persons unknown. It was Korten, the young public prosecutor who, in an impassioned plea for freedom of the press and the right to protect the identity of sources of information, stressed that a person who did not keep or fall into bad company could obviously never give the press cause for wild and potentially damaging reporting.

The whole affair – that was to say, the sudden appearance of Götten and of the shadowy figure of Karl, the man dressed as a sheikh – did, Korten must say, imply a strange casualness in social intercourse. This had not as yet been adequately explained to him, and he was counting on receiving plausible explanations during the interrogation of the two young ladies concerned. She, Miss Woltersheim, could not escape the reproach of having been less than fastidious in the choice of her guests. Miss Woltersheim refused to be taken to task in this way by a person considerably younger than herself, and pointed out that she had invited the two girls each to bring a friend, and that she must say it was not her custom to ask her guests for their friends' identification papers or a police certificate of good conduct; whereupon she was rebuked and told that in this instance age was not a factor whereas the status of the public prosecutor, Mr Korten, was, and a very considerable one at that. She must realize that the matter now under investigation was a serious one, a grave, if not the gravest, case of crime by violence, in which Götten, as the evidence showed, was involved. She must leave it to the state's legal representative to decide which details and which admonishments were appropriate.

When asked once again whether Götten and the gentleman visitor could be one and the same person, Miss Woltersheim said No, there was absolutely no possibility of that. But then when she was asked whether she knew the 'gentleman visitor' personally, whether she had ever seen him or ever met him, she had to reply in the negative, and since she had also been unaware of such an important personal detail as the mysterious automobile drives her testimony was termed unsatisfactory, and for the time being she was dismissed 'on a sour note'. Before leaving the room, obviously annoyed, she further declared that Karl, the man dressed as a sheikh, had seemed to her at least as suspicious as Götten. In any event, he had kept talking to himself while in the washroom and had then disappeared without saying good-bye.

29

Since it was Hertha Scheumel, a salesgirl, aged seventeen, who had brought Götten to the party, she was the next to be interrogated. She was obviously nervous, saying she had never had anything to do with the police before, but then proceeded to offer a relatively plausible explanation for knowing Götten. 'I live,' she stated, 'with my girl friend Claudia Sterm, who works in a chocolate factory, in a one-room apartment with kitchen and shower. We both come from Kuir-Oftersbroich and are both distantly related to Miss Woltersheim as well as to Katharina Blum' (although Miss Scheumel wished to describe the remoteness of the relationship in more detail by mentioning grandparents who had been cousins of grandparents, a precise degree of relationship was not deemed necessary and the term 'distant' was regarded as adequate). 'We call Miss Woltersheim Auntie and think of Katharina as a cousin.

'That evening, Wednesday, 20 February 1974, we were both, Claudia and I, in a real bind. We had promised Auntie Else to bring our boyfriends to her dance as otherwise there wouldn't be enough men to go around. Well, it so happened that my boyfriend, who is doing his military service in the Army at the moment, or, to be more exact, with the Engineers, has suddenly — as usual — been assigned to barracks duty, and although I suggested he simply take off I couldn't persuade him, because he'd already done that a few times and was scared of getting into real trouble. As for Claudia's boyfriend, by early afternoon he was so drunk we had to put him to bed. So we decided to go to the Café Polkt and pick up a couple of nice fellows there, since we didn't want to lose face with Auntie. There's always something going on at the café during Carnival time. People meet there before and after dances and the Carnival ceremonies, and you can always be sure of finding lots of young people there.

'By late Wednesday afternoon the atmosphere at the café was already pretty good. I was twice asked to dance by this young man, and by the way I have only just learned that his name is Ludwig Götten and that he's a wanted criminal, and during the second dance I asked him if he wouldn't like to go to a party with me. He seemed delighted and agreed at once. He said he was just passing through, had no place to stay and no idea how he was going to spend the evening, and he would like to come with me very much. At the very moment when I was, you might say, fixing up a date with this Götten, Claudia happened to be dancing next to me with a man dressed as a sheikh, and I suppose they must have overheard what we were saying because the sheikh, who I learned later was called Karl, at once asked Claudia, in a kind of humble way which was meant to be funny, whether we couldn't find some small corner for him at this party as well, he was lonesome too and had no plans for the evening.

'Anyway, we'd got what we were after, and soon after that we drove in Ludwig's – I mean Mr Götten's – car to Auntie Else's apartment. It was a Porsche, not very comfortable for four, but then we didn't have far to go. If I was asked whether Katharina Blum knew we were going to the Café Polkt to pick up a couple of fellows, I'd answer Yes. I had called her that morning at the Blornas, where she works, and told her that Claudia and I would have to go alone if we couldn't find anybody. I also told her we were going to the Café Polkt. She didn't think that was a good idea, she said we were too gullible, too irresponsible. But then we all know Katharina's funny about such things. That's why I was so surprised when Katharina grabbed hold of Götten almost immediately and danced with him the whole evening, as if they'd known each other all their lives.'

30

Hertha Scheumel's statement was confirmed almost word for word by her friend Claudia Sterm. There was only one point, an insignificant one, in which they differed. She said she had danced three times, not twice, with the sheikh, because Karl had asked her to dance earlier than Götten had asked Hertha. And Claudia Sterm also expressed surprise at how quickly Katharina, who was always considered so standoffish, had become friendly, you might almost say familiar, with Götten.

31

There were three further guests at the party to be interrogated: Konrad Beiters, aged fifty-six, textile agent and friend of Miss Woltersheim's, and Mr Georg Plotten (aged forty-two) and his wife Hedwig (aged thirty-six), both municipal employees. All three agreed in their account of the evening, from the arrival of Katharina Blum, of Hertha Scheumel accompanied by Ludwig Götten, and of Claudia Sterm accompanied by Karl in his sheikh costume. Furthermore, it had been a very nice evening, with dancing, and general conversation in which Karl had turned out to be especially amusing. The only wrong note – if you could call it that, for no doubt those two hadn't felt it to be one – was, according to Georg Plotten, the 'total monopoly of Katharina Blum by Ludwig Götten'. It had lent a serious, almost solemn note to the evening, something that wasn't too well suited to Carnival parties. Mrs Hedwig Plotten stated that, after the departure of Katharina and Ludwig, when she had gone into the kitchen to get some more ice, she too had noticed Karl the sheikh talking to himself in the washroom. Moreover, this Karl had left shortly afterward, without saying good-bye.

32

Katharina Blum, brought back for questioning, confirmed her telephone conversation with Hertha Scheumel but persisted in her denial that it had concerned any arrangement for a meeting with Götten, for it was suggested to her – not by Beizmenne but by Korten, the younger of the two prosecutors – that she would do well to admit that Götten had called her up after her telephone conversation with Hertha Scheumel, and that she had been smart enough to send Götten to the Café Polkt and have him get into conversation with Hertha Scheumel so that he could meet her (Katharina) at Miss Woltersheim's without attracting attention. This had been easy enough to do since Miss Scheumel was a striking blonde, somewhat flashily dressed. Katharina Blum, by now almost totally apathetic, merely shook her head as she sat there still clutching the two issues of the *News*. She was then dismissed and, together with Miss Woltersheim and Konrad Beiters, left police headquarters.

33

In discussing the signed depositions and rechecking them for possible gaps, Korten raised the question of whether some serious effort should not be made to bring in this sheikh by the name of Karl and investigate his highly obscure role in the affair. He must say he was very surprised that no measures had been taken to trace this 'Karl'. After all, this Karl had obviously turned up simultaneously, if not together, with Götten at the Café Polkt and had likewise 'crashed' the party, and to him – Korten – his role appeared mysterious if not suspicious.

At this point all those present burst out laughing; even the normally reserved Policewoman Pletzer permitted herself a smile. The stenographer, Mrs Anna Lockster, laughed so raucously that she had to be called to order by Beizmenne. And finally, since Korten still had not understood, his colleague Hach enlightened him. Had Korten not realized, or noticed, that Commissioner Beizmenne had deliberately passed over or failed to mention the sheikh?

Surely it was obvious that he was 'one of our men' and that the alleged monologue in the washroom was nothing more than a method – clumsily executed, it was true – of instructing his colleagues by pocket transmitter to start shadowing Götten and Blum, for of course by this time Blum's address was known. 'And no doubt you also realize, Mr Korten, that during Carnival time sheikh costumes are the ideal disguise, since nowadays, for obvious reasons, sheikhs are more popular than cowboys.' And Beizmenne added: 'Of course, we realized right away that the Carnival would make it easier for the lawbreakers to drop out of sight and more difficult for us to remain hot on the trail, Götten having been tailed for the past thirty-six hours. Götten – who, by the way, was not disguised – had spent the night in a VW bus on the parking lot from which he later stole the Porsche, and he had breakfast in a café where he then shaved and changed in the washroom. We didn't lose sight of him for a single minute, we had about a dozen policemen disguised as sheikhs, cowboys, and Spaniards on his tail, all equipped with pocket transmitters and acting like revellers somewhat the worse for wear, ready to report instantly on any attempts at contact. The persons Götten contacted before entering the Café Polkt have all been traced and checked out:

a bartender at whose counter he had a beer;
two girls with whom he danced at a nightclub in the old quarter of the town;
a gas-station attendant near the Holzmarkt who filled up the stolen Porsche;
a man at the news-stand on Matthias-Strasse;
a sales clerk (male) in a tobacco store;
a bank teller at whose window he changed seven hundred U.S. dollars which probably originated from a bank holdup.

'All these persons have been identified unequivocally as chance encounters rather than planned contacts, and none of the words exchanged with each individual person suggests a code. However, I will not be persuaded that Miss Blum was also a chance encounter. Her telephone conversation with Miss Scheumel, the punctuality with which she turned up at Miss Woltersheim's, and that damned intimacy with which the two of them danced right from the very first second – and the speed with which they made off together – everything speaks against chance. But, above all, the fact that she apparently let him leave without saying good-bye and quite obviously showed him a way out of the apartment building that must have been overlooked by our strict surveillance. The apartment building – that is, the building within the apartment complex where she lives – was never out of our sight for one moment. Of course, we could not keep the entire area of almost one and a half square kilometres under complete surveillance. She must have known an escape route and shown it to him; besides, I am certain that she found a hideout for him – and possibly others too – and knows exactly where he is. The buildings of her employers have already been checked out, we have made inquiries in her own village, and Miss Woltersheim's apartment has again been thoroughly searched while she was here for questioning. Nothing. In my opinion the best thing would be to let her run around freely so she can make a mistake, and probably the trail will lead to his present quarters via that mysterious gentleman visitor, and I am certain that the trail to the escape route inside the apartment building leads via Mrs Blorna, whom we now know also as "Trude the Red" and who was one of the architects who designed the apartment complex.'

34

This brings us to the end of the first backing-up process, we have moved from the Friday to the Saturday. Everything will be done to avoid further blockages and unnecessary build-ups of tension. It will probably not be possible to avoid them entirely.

However, it may be illuminating to note that, after the final interrogation on Friday afternoon, Katharina Blum asked Else Woltersheim and Konrad Beiters to drive her first to her apartment and – please, please – to go up with her. She told them she was scared: during that Thursday night, shortly after her telephone conversation with Götten (any outsider should recognize her innocence from the fact that she spoke openly, although not while being questioned, about her telephone contacts with Götten!) something absolutely revolting had happened. Almost immediately after her call from Götten, in fact she had hardly replaced the receiver, the phone rang again, and in the 'wild hope' that it was Götten again she had at once picked up the receiver, but instead of Götten on the line it had been a 'horribly soft' male voice 'whispering' a whole string of 'nasty things' to her, wicked things, and the worst of it was that the fellow had said he lived in the same building and why, if she was so keen on intimacies, did she look for them so far away, he was willing and able to offer her every conceivable variety of intimacy. Yes, it was because of this phone call that she had gone to Else's that same night. She was scared, scared of the phone even, and, since Götten had her phone number although she didn't have Götten's, she was still hoping for a call while at the same time being scared of the phone.

Well, we must not withhold the fact that there were more scares in store for Katharina Blum. To begin with: her mailbox, which so far had played a very insignificant role in her life and which she generally glanced into simply 'because everyone does' but without success. On this Friday morning it was full to overflowing, and in a manner far from delighting Katharina. For, although Else W. and Beiters did their utmost to intercept her mail, she would not be deterred and, presumably in the hope of some sign of life from her dear Ludwig, looked through all the letters and circulars – totalling about twenty – evidently without finding anything from Ludwig, and stuffed the whole bundle into her handbag. Even the ride up in the elevator was an ordeal since two other occupants of the building were riding up too. One man (it must be said, improbable though it may sound) dressed as a sheikh, who squeezed himself into a corner in an agony of attempted dissociation but fortunately got out at the fourth floor; and a woman (what's true is true, crazy though it may sound) dressed as an Andalusian, and this person, protected by her mask, far from moving away from Katharina remained standing directly beside her, looking her up and down with brazen curiosity out of 'impudent, hard brown eyes'. She continued up beyond the eighth floor.

Warning: there is worse to come. When she had finally reached her apartment, clinging to Beiters and Miss W. as she walked in, the telephone rang, and here Miss W. was quicker than Katharina: shaking off Katharina she ran to pick up the receiver, they saw her horrified expression, saw her turn pale, heard her 'You filthy bitch, you filthy cowardly bitch', and instead of replacing the receiver she craftily put it down beside the cradle.

In vain did Miss W. and Beiters try to part Katharina from her mail: she kept the bundle of letters and circulars firmly clutched in her hands, together with the two issues of the *News* that she had also taken from her bag, and insisted on opening it all. It was useless. She read every one!

Not all of it was anonymous. One letter that was not anonymous – the most detailed – came from a firm calling itself 'Mail Orders Intimate' and offering her every variety of sex article. For a person of Katharina's sensibility, this was pretty strong stuff, and even worse was that someone had written by hand in the margin: *'These* are the genuine articles!' In short – or, better still, in statistical terms – the other eighteen items of mail were:

seven anonymous postcards, handwitten with 'crude' sexual propositions that in one way or another all included the words 'Communist bitch';

four more anonymous postcards containing insulting political remarks but no sexual propositions. These marks ranged from 'Red agitator' to 'Kremlin stooge';

five letters containing clippings from the *News*, most of which (some three or four) had comments written in red ink in the margins such as: 'Where Stalin failed, you'll fail too';

two letters containing religious exhortations, and on the tracts enclosed with them was written: 'You must learn to pray again, you poor lost child', and 'Kneel down and confess, God has not yet abandoned you.'

And only now did Else W. discover a piece of paper that had been pushed under the door and which fortunately she was able to hide from Katharina: 'Why don't you make use of my sex catalogue? Do I have to force your happiness on you? Your neighbour, whom you have so haughtily rejected. I am warning you.' This had been printed in script from which Else W. thought she could deduce a college education if not medical training.

35

It is, surely, astonishing that neither Miss W. nor Konrad B. was astonished when, with no thought of intervening in any way, they watched Katharina walk to the little bar in her living room, take out one bottle each of sherry, whisky, and red wine and a half-empty bottle of cherry syrup and, with no visible sign of emotion, throw them against the immaculate walls, where they smashed and spewed their contents.

She did the same in her little kitchen, using tomato ketchup, salad dressing, vinegar, and Worcester sauce for the same purpose. Must we add that she did the same in her bathroom with tubes and jars of face cream, powder, and bath oil – and in her bedroom with a bottle of eau de cologne?

Through it all she appeared so systematic, so impassive, so convinced and convincing, that Else W. and Konrad B. never lifted a finger.

36

Naturally there have been a good many theories aimed at pinpointing the exact moment in time at which Katharina first formed her intention to commit a murder or devised her plan for murder and decided to carry it out. Some people think that first article in Thursday's *News* did the trick; others regard Friday as the crucial day because that day the *News* was still stirring up trouble and destroying (subjectively, at least) her neighbourhood and the apartment of which she was so fond; then came the anonymous caller, the anonymous mail – and to cap it all the *News* of Saturday, plus (here we are looking ahead!) the *Sunday News*. Surely such speculations are idle: she planned the murder and carried it out – and that's that! Without a doubt something in her 'came to a head' – the statements of her former husband particularly upset her, and we can be certain that the contents of the *Sunday News*, if not actually the trigger, must have had a far from soothing effect on her.

37

Before our flashback may be regarded as complete and we can focus once again on Saturday, it remains necessary to describe Friday evening and Friday night at Miss Woltersheim's. Overall conclusion: surprisingly peaceful. True, attempts by Konrad Beiters to distract Katharina by putting on some dance records, even Latin American ones, and asking her to dance were not a success, nor was the attempt to part Katharina from the *News* and her anonymous mail; attempts to make out that the whole thing wasn't all that important and would soon pass also came to nothing. She'd been through worse, hadn't she? Her miserable childhood, her marriage with that wretch Brettloh, the alcoholism and, 'to put it mildly, the depravity of your mother who, when all's said and done, is responsible for Kurt's leaving the straight and narrow.' Wasn't Götten safe, at least for the time being, and his promise to come for her to be taken seriously? Wasn't it Carnival, and wasn't her financial position secure? Weren't there all those nice people like the Blornas and the Hiepertzes, and wasn't even that 'conceited jackass' – there was still some reluctance to name the gentleman visitor by name – actually quite an amusing character and far from sinister?

Katharina would have none of this and reminded them of the 'stupid ring and that silly fancy envelope' that had got them both into such a terrible jam and might even have brought suspicion on Ludwig. Could she ever have known that that jackass would spend all that money for the sake of his vanity? No, indeed, she certainly couldn't call him amusing. No.

When they turned to practical matters – whether, for instance, she should look for a new apartment and whether it wasn't time to discuss where – Katharina became evasive, saying the only practical matter she had in mind was to make herself a Carnival costume, and she asked Else to lend her a big sheet since, in view of the vogue for sheikhs, she intended to 'join the crowds' on Saturday or Sunday dressed as a Bedouin woman. So what's happened that is so bad? Scarcely a thing, if you look at it closely or, to be more precise: almost everything has been good, for isn't it a fact that Katharina has met 'the One who was to come', hasn't she 'spent a night of romance' with him? Granted, she has been questioned, or rather interrogated, and it is clear that Ludwig is no mere 'butterfly hunter'. Then there has been the usual filth in the *News*, a few filthy beasts have made anonymous phone calls, others have written anonymous letters. But doesn't life go on? Isn't Ludwig being well – in fact comfortably – provided for, as she and only she knows? Now we're fixing up a Carnival costume which will make Katharina look delightful, a white burnous; how pretty she'll look when she 'joins the crowds' in it!

Finally even Nature demands her due, and one falls asleep, dozes off, wakes up again, dozes off again. How about a little drink? Why not? Peace and quiet reign: a young woman fallen asleep over her sewing while an older man

69

and woman move cautiously around her 'so as not to interfere with Nature'. Nature is so little interfered with that
Katharina is not even roused by the telephone when it rings
around two-thirty in the morning. Why do the hands of
sober Else Woltersheim start trembling as she lifts the
receiver? Is she expecting anonymous intimacies such as she
heard a few hours ago? Mind you, two-thirty in the morning
is an alarming hour for anyone to call, but she grabs the
receiver, which Beiters snatches from her, and when he says
'Yes?' the receiver at the other end is replaced immediately.
And it rings again, and again – the moment he picks it up,
even before he says 'Yes?' – the caller replaces the receiver.
Naturally there are people who want to turn a person into a
nervous wreck once they've got one's name and address from
the *News*, and the best thing is not to replace the receiver.

And at that point it is decided to shield Katharina at least
from the Saturday edition of the *News*; but Katharina has
taken advantage of a few moments while Else W. is asleep
and Konrad B. is shaving in the bathroom, and she has crept
out on to the street, where in the early-morning light she has
flung open the first *News*box she comes to and committed a
kind of sacrilege: she has abused the CONFIDENCE of the
News by taking a *News*paper without paying for it! At this
juncture our flashback may be considered temporarily complete, this being the very hour at which the Blornas, this
same Saturday, travel-worn, irritable, and depressed, leave
the night train and pick up that same edition of the *News*,
to be studied when they get home.

38

At the Blorna home it is a depressing Saturday morning, extremely depressing in fact, not only because of an almost sleepless night of being rattled and jolted about in the sleeper, not only because of the *News*, which, to quote Mrs Blorna, pursues one like the plague wherever one goes, one isn't safe anywhere; depressing not only because of the reproachful telegrams sent by influential friends, business acquaintances, and 'Lüstra' (LÜding & STRÄubleder Investments) but also because of Hach, whom they call too early in the day, too early, that's all (and yet too late when they reflect that they would have done better to call him on Thursday). He could hardly be described as cordial, told them that Katharina's interrogation was over, couldn't say whether proceedings would be taken against her, at the moment she certainly needed support but so far not legal support. Had they forgotten it was Carnival and that even public prosecutors had the right to some free time and a bit of celebrating? Well, of course, they had known each other for twenty-four years, had been at university together, crammed together, sung together, even hiked together, and one is not going to let a few minutes of grumpiness upset one, especially since one is feeling so extremely depressed oneself, but then came the request – and from a public prosecutor! – to continue the discussion in person rather than over the long-distance phone. Yes, there was a certain amount of incriminating evidence against her, there was much that needed explaining, but no more now, maybe later that afternoon, when they could be together. Where? In town. They would walk up and down somewhere, that would be best. In the lobby of the museum. At four-thirty. No phone calls to Katharina's apartment, none to Miss Woltersheim, none to Mr and Mrs Hiepertz.

It was also depressing to find that the absence of Katharina's orderly hand made itself felt with such speed and clarity. How in the world did it happen that within half an hour – though all they had done was to make some coffee, get out some rye crisp, butter, and honey, and place their few pieces of baggage in the hall – chaos seemed already to have broken loose, and finally even Trude became irritable because he kept on asking her how she could possibly see any connection between Katharina's affair and Alois Sträubleder, let alone Lüding, and she didn't do a thing to help him, merely pointing, in her mock naive-ironic way, which at other times he liked but did not appreciate at all this morning, to the two issues of the *News*, and hadn't he been struck by one phrase in particular, and when he asked her what phrase she refused to tell him, remarking sarcastically that she wanted to test his perspicuity, and he read 'this filth, this damn filth, that pursues a person wherever he goes', over and over again, not concentrating because the anger over his twisted statement and 'Trude the Red' kept mounting in him afresh, until he finally capitulated and humbly asked Trude to help him out; he was so beside himself, he said, that his perspicuity failed him; besides, for years he had been only a corporation lawyer, had done scarcely any criminal work at all, to which she replied dryly, 'Too bad,' but then showed some mercy by saying, 'You mean you didn't notice the phrase "gentleman visitor", or that I connected that phrase with the telegrams? Would anyone ever describe this Götting – no, Götten – just have a good look at his pictures again, would anyone ever describe him, no matter how he was dressed, as a "gentleman visitor"? No, you must agree that someone like that would only be called a "male visitor" in the language of amateur

72

informers living in the building, and I'll turn myself into a prophet here and now and tell you that within one hour at the most we shall also be receiving a gentleman visitor, and another thing I'll prophesy is: trouble, confrontation – and possibly the end of an old friendship, trouble too with your Trude the Red and more than trouble with Katharina, who has two fatal characteristics: loyalty and pride, and she will never, never admit that she showed this boy an escape route, one which we – she and I had looked over together. Take it easy, dear heart, take it easy: it'll never come out, but to tell the truth I'm the one responsible for this Götting, no Götten, vanishing from her apartment without being seen. I don't suppose you remember, but I had a diagram of the entire heating, ventilation, plumbing, and cable systems of "Elegant Riverside Residences" hanging in my bedroom. It showed the heating ducts in red, the ventilation ducts in blue, the cables in green, and the plumbing in yellow. This diagram fascinated Katharina to such a degree – and you know what a person she is for order and planning, in fact she's positively brilliant at it – that she would stand in front of it for a long time and keep asking me about the relationships and significance of this "abstract painting" as she called it, and I was just about to get hold of a copy and give it to her. I'm rather relieved I didn't, imagine if they'd found a copy of the diagram in her apartment – that would have been the best kind of support for the conspiracy theory, the idea of an arms depot, the link between "Trude-the-Red-and-outlaws" and "Katharina-and-gentleman-visitor". Naturally a diagram like that would be an ideal guide for all kinds of intruders – burglars, lovers, whatever – who wanted to come and go without being seen. I even explained the height of the various passages to her: where you can walk upright, where you have to duck, where you have to crawl, when pipes burst or cables break down. This is the only possible way our fine young gentleman, whose caresses she can now only dream about, can have slipped through the police, and if he's really a bank robber he'll have tumbled to the system at once. Maybe that's how the gentleman visitor went in and out too. These modern apartment blocks require totally different methods of surveillance from the old-fashioned apartment buildings. Sometime or other you must tip off the police and the public prosecutor's office. They watch the main entrances, and possibly the lobby and elevator, but there's also a service elevator leading directly to the basement – and there a person can crawl a few hundred yards, lift up a manhole cover somewhere, and vanish into thin air. Believe me, there's nothing to do now but pray, for the last thing Alois needs is *News* headlines in any shape or form. What he needs now is for the findings and the reports on them to be thoroughly doctored, and what he's just as scared of as headlines is the sourpuss expression of one Maud, his well and truly wedded wife, by whom, incidentally, he has four children. You mean to say you've never noticed how "boyishly gay", how "high-spirited", he was – and, I must say, he couldn't have been nicer the few times he danced with Katharina, and how he positively insisted on driving her home – and how boyishly disappointed he was when she got her own car? The very thing he needed, the very thing his heart desired – an exceptionally nice young person like Katharina, not "fast" and yet – what do you men call it? – with a capacity for love, serious and yet young, and prettier than she ever realized. Hasn't she sometimes gladdened your manly heart a bit?'

Yes, of course she had: gladdened his manly heart, and he admitted it, and also admitted that he did more, much more, than just like her, and she, Trude, must know that everyone, not only men, sometimes had strange impulses just to take someone in their arms, and maybe more – but

Katharina, no, there was something about her that could never, never have made him one of her gentlemen visitors, and if something had held him back, indeed made it impossible for him to become – or should he say, try to become – one it wasn't, and she knew how he meant this, it wasn't respect for her, Trude, or consideration for her, but respect for Katharina – that was it, respect, you might say reverence, more, *fond* reverence for her, hell, innocence – and more, more than innocence, something he couldn't find the right word for. It must be that strange, warmhearted reserve of Katharina's and – although he was fifteen years her senior and God knew he had done pretty well in life – the way Katharina had set to work to plan and organize her ruined life – it was this that had held him back, if he had ever had any such ideas, because he had been afraid of destroying her or her life – she was so vulnerable, so damn vulnerable, and if it turned out that Alois actually had been her gentleman visitor he would – to put it plainly – 'punch him in the jaw'; yes, they must help, help her, those tricks and interrogations and questionings were more than she could handle – and now it was too late, and somehow or other he must find Katharina before the day was out . . . but at this point he was interrupted in his revelatory musings by Trude remarking, in her inimitable wry manner: 'The gentleman visitor has just driven up.'

39

It must be established here and now that Blorna did not punch Sträubleder in the jaw, although indeed it was he driving up in a flashy rented car. It is our wish not only that as little blood should flow here as possible, but also that the portrayal of physical violence, if it must be mentioned at all, should be kept to the minimum required by our reportorial obligations. This does not mean that the atmosphere at the Blornas became less depressing; on the contrary, it became more depressing than ever, for Trude B. could not resist greeting their old friend, as she went on stirring her coffee, with the words: 'Hello there, gentleman visitor.' 'I assume,' said Blorna in embarrassment, 'that Trude has once again hit the nail on the head.' 'Yes,' said Sträubleder, 'I just wonder whether that's always so tactful.'

Here it may be noted that the relationship between Mrs Blorna and Alois Sträubleder had once become almost unbearably strained when he had tried, if not exactly to seduce her, certainly to make a pass at her and she in her dry way had given him to understand that, irresistible though he might be in his own eyes, he was not so in hers. In these circumstances it will be understood why Blorna escorted Sträubleder immediately to his study and asked his wife to leave them alone together and in the interval ('interval between what?' asked Mrs Blorna) to make every possible effort to locate Katharina.

40

Why does one suddenly find one's own study so repulsive, everything upside down and dirty although there is not a speck of dust to be seen and everything is in its proper place? What makes the red leather armchairs, in which one has clinched many a good business deal and had many a confidential chat, in which one can be really relaxed and listen to music, suddenly seem so repulsive, even the bookshelves disgusting and the signed Chagall on the wall downright suspect, as if it were a fake done by the artist himself? Ashtrays, lighters, whisky decanter – what makes one dislike these harmless if expensive objects? What makes such a depressing day after an extremely depressing night so intolerable and the tension between old friends so powerful that sparks are ready to fly? Why does one dislike the walls, stippled in soft yellow and adorned with contemporary graphic art?

'It's like this,' said Alois Sträubleder, 'I really only came to tell you that I no longer need your help in *this* affair. You lost your nerve again, out there at the airport in the fog. An hour after you both lost your nerve or your patience the fog lifted, and you could still have been here by 6.30 in the evening. If you'd thought it over quietly, you could have called the airport in Munich and found out that flights were leaving on time again. But never mind about that. To be perfectly honest with you – even if there'd been no fog and the plane *had* left on time, you'd have got here too late because the crucial part of the questioning was over long before and there'd have been nothing left for you to prevent.'

'I'm no match for the *News* anyway,' said Blorna.

'The *News*,' said Sträubleder, 'is no threat, Lüding's seen to that, but there are other papers, and I don't mind any kind of headline except this kind that associates me with outlaws. If an affair with a woman gets me into trouble, it's private trouble, not public. Even a picture of me with a woman as attractive as Katharina Blum wouldn't harm me, and by the way they're dropping the theory of the male visitor, and neither the ring nor the letter – well yes, I did give her a rather valuable ring, which they've found, and I did write her a few letters, of which all they've found is one envelope – neither of those things is going to present a problem. The bad part is that this Tötges uses a different name when he writes things for the weeklies which the *News* is not allowed to print, and that – well – Katharina has promised him an exclusive interview. I just found this out a few minutes ago, from Lüding, what's more he's glad Tötges is taking up the offer since, as I say, the *News* has been taken care of, but we've no influence on Tötges's other journalistic activities, he handles those through a go-between. You don't seem to be in the picture at all, do you?'

'I've no idea what's going on,' said Blorna.

'An odd state of affairs for an attorney whose client I am, I must say; that comes from frittering away one's time in rattling trains instead of getting in touch with weather bureaux which could have told one that the fog would soon lift. So you haven't been in touch with her yet?'

'No, have you?'

'No, not directly. I only know that about an hour ago she called the *News* and promised Tötges an exclusive interview for tomorrow afternoon. He accepted. And there's something else that worries me more, much much more, it's tying my stomach in knots' (here Sträubleder's face showed something like emotion and his voice became strained), 'starting tomorrow you can say what you like about me, and as much as you like, because it's true that I've abused your confidence and Trude's – but on the other hand we do live in a free country where it's permitted to lead a free love life, and you must believe me when I say I would do anything to help her, I would even gamble my reputation, for – go ahead, laugh – I love that woman, but: she's beyond helping – *I* can still use some help – she simply won't let herself be helped ...'

'And is there no way you can help her, protect her from the *News*, from those bastards?'

'Now listen, you mustn't take that business with the *News* so seriously, even if they have rather got their claws into you and Trude. For God's sake let's not quarrel now over the yellow press and the freedom of the press. I'll come to the point: I'd appreciate it if you could be present at the interview as my attorney *and* hers. You see, the really devastating part still hasn't come out either in the interrogations or in the press: six months ago I induced her to accept a key to our country place in Kohlforstenheim. They didn't find the key when they searched either the house or Katharina, but she *has* it, or at least she did have it, if she hasn't just thrown it away. It was just a sentimental impulse on my part, call it what you like, but I wanted her to have a key to the house because I refused to give up hope that she would come to me there one day. You must believe that I would help her, that I'd stand by her, that I'd even go to them and confess: Look, *I'm* the mysterious visitor – but I know only too well: while she'd let me down, she'd never let down that Ludwig of hers.'

There was something quite new, unexpected, in Sträubleder's expression, something that aroused, if not pity, at least curiosity in Blorna; it was a kind of humility, or was it jealousy?

'What's all this about jewellery and letters and now a key?'

'For God's sake, Hubert, don't you get it yet? It's something I can't tell either Lüding or Hach or the police – I'm convinced she's given the key to that fellow Ludwig and that that's where he's been hiding out the past two days. I'm scared, I tell you, about Katharina, about the police, and about that young idiot too who may be hiding out in my house in Kohlforstenheim. I'd like him to disappear before they find him, but at the same time I'd like them to catch him, to put an end to the whole business. Now do you get it? What's your advice?'

'You might call up there, in Kohlforstenheim, it seems to me.'

'And do you really believe that if he's there he'll answer the phone?'

'All right, then you must call the police, there's no alternative. If only to prevent a disaster. Call them anonymously, if you must. If there's even the slightest possibility that Götten is at your place out there, you must notify the police immediately. Otherwise I will.'

'So that my house and name get linked up in the headlines with that outlaw after all? I had a different idea ... I was thinking maybe you could drive out there, I mean to Kohlforstenheim, as my attorney, sort of, just to make sure the place is all right.'

'At this moment in time? On Carnival Saturday, with the *News* already aware that I've abruptly broken off my vacation – and I'm supposed to have done that just to make sure everything's all right at your place in the country? The fridge still working, hm? The thermostat still set properly, no windows smashed, enough liquor in the bar and the sheets not damp? And for that an eminent corporation lawyer, owner of a luxury villa with a swimming pool and married to "Trude the Red", comes rushing back from his vacation? Do you really think that's such a smart idea, when we may be certain that the gentlemen from the *News* are watching my every move – and there I go driving, straight from the sleeper as it were, out to your country home to see if the crocuses will soon be peeking through or the snowdrops are already out? Do you really think that's such a great idea – quite apart from the fact that our friend Ludwig has already proved he's a pretty good shot?'

'Hell, I'm not sure whether your wisecracks are so appropriate right now. I ask you, as my attorney and my friend, to render me a service, and not even an especially personal one at that, really more a kind of citizen's duty – and you come back at me with snowdrops. Since yesterday this affair's been kept so secret that we haven't had so much as a grain of information out of them since this morning. All we know is what we read in the *News*, and we're lucky that Lüding has enough pull there. The public prosecutor's office and the police have even stopped calling the Ministry of the Interior, and Lüding has pull there too. It's a matter of life and death, Hubert.'

Just then Trude entered without knocking, carrying the transistor radio and saying quietly: 'No longer of death, only of life, thank God. They've caught the boy, he was stupid enough to shoot and so they shot at him, he's wounded but in no danger. In your garden, Alois, out in Kohlforstenheim, between the swimming pool and the pergola. They describe it as the super-luxury villa of one of Lüding's cronies. Incidentally, there's still such a thing as a true gentleman: the first thing our friend Ludwig said was that Katharina had absolutely nothing to do with the whole business, it was a purely private love affair totally unrelated to the crimes with which he was charged but which he continued to deny. You'll probably have to have a few windows replaced, Alois – they banged around there quite a bit. Your name hasn't cropped up yet, but maybe you should call Maud, she must be upset and in need of consolation. By the way, they caught three of Götten's alleged accomplices at the same time, in other places. The whole thing is called a triumph for a certain Commissioner Beizmenne. And now get going, Alois my dear, and this time call on your wife for a change – maybe she could do with a gentleman visitor.'

It is not hard to imagine that at this point Blorna's study came close to being the scene of a physical confrontation definitely not in keeping with the surroundings and furnishings of the room. Sträubleder allegedly – *allegedly* – flew at Trude's throat but was prevented by her husband, who pointed out to him that surely he did not intend to attack a lady. Sträubleder allegedly – *allegedly* – said that he wasn't sure whether the term 'lady' applied to such a shrew, and there were some words that in certain circumstances, and especially in the wake of tragic events, should not be used sarcastically, and those words were loaded, and if he heard them once more, just once more, then – yes, what then – well, that would be the end. He had scarcely left the house and Blorna had had no chance to tell Trude that maybe she *had* gone a bit far when she cut in with: 'Katharina's mother died last night. I did manage to locate her: she's in Kuir-Hochsackel.'

41

Before embarking on our final diversion and rerouting manoeuvres we must be permitted to make the following 'technical' interjection. Too much is happening in this story. To an embarrassing, almost ungovernable degree, it is pregnant with action: to its disadvantage. Naturally it is to be deplored when a self-employed housekeeper shoots and kills a reporter, and a case of this kind undoubtedly has to be cleared up or at least an attempt must be made to do so. But what is to be done with successful attorneys who break off their hard-earned ski-ing vacations for the sake of a housekeeper? With industrialists (who are professors and politicos on the side) who in their callow sentimental way simply force keys to country homes (and themselves) on this housekeeper, in both cases unavailingly, as we know, and who want publicity but only of a certain kind; with a whole raft of objects and people whom it is impossible to synchronize and who continually disturb the flow (i.e., the linear course of events), because they are, shall we say, immune? What is to be done with crime commissioners who continually, and successfully, demand 'little plugs'? In a nutshell: it is all too full of holes, and yet, at what is for the narrator the crucial moment, not full enough, because, while it is possible to learn of this or that (from Hach, maybe, and a few male and female police officials), nothing, absolutely nothing of what they say holds water because it would never be confirmed by or even stated in a court of law. It is not conclusive evidence! It has not the slightest public value.

For example, this whole business of 'little plugs'. Of course, wiretapping yields information, but that very information – since the tapping is carried out by other than the investigating authorities – not only may not be used in public proceedings, it may not even be mentioned. Above all: what goes on in the 'psyche' of the wiretapper? What passes through the mind of a blameless civil servant who is only doing his duty, who, we might say, is required to do his duty (albeit reluctantly) by the exigencies of earning a living if not of obedience to orders? What does he think when obliged to monitor a telephone conversation between that unknown apartment dweller, whom we will designate here the hawker of intimacies, and such an unusually nice, smart, virtually blameless person as Katharina Blum? Does he find himself in a state of moral or sexual excitement, or both? Does he become indignant, feel pity, or even derive some weird pleasure from a person nicknamed 'the nun' being wounded in the depths of her soul by hoarse and menacing propositions?

With all this happening in the foreground, even more is going on in the background. What does a harmless wiretapper who is merely doing his job think when a certain Lüding, who has been mentioned here from time to time, calls up the editor in chief of the *News* and says something like: 'S. right out, as of now, and B. in?' Naturally Lüding is not being tapped because *he* has to be kept under observation, but because of the threat that someone – blackmailer, politician, gangster, etc. – may call *him* up. How is a blameless monitor to know that S. stands for Sträubleder and B. for Blorna, and that readers of the *Sunday News* will find nothing more about S. but a great deal about B.? And yet – who is to know or even suspect this? – Blorna is an attorney of whom Lüding has the highest opinion, one who time and again has proved his skill at both the national and international level. When elsewhere we speak of sources that 'can never come together', all we are thinking of is the song about the prince and the princess whose candle is blown out by the false nun – and someone fell into rather deep water and drowned.

And Mrs Lüding tells her cook to call her husband's secretary and find out what kind of dessert Lüding would like on Sunday: crêpes with poppy seed? Strawberries with ice cream *and* whipped cream, or with ice cream only or with whipped cream only? Whereupon the secretary, who would rather not disturb her boss but knows his tastes yet on the other hand may merely want to cause trouble, tells the cook with some asperity that she is convinced that this Sunday Mr Lüding would prefer *crème brûlée*. The cook, who of course also knows Lüding's tastes, refuses to accept this, saying this is news to her and is the secretary sure she is not confusing her own tastes with those of Mr Lüding, and would she kindly put her through so she can talk to Mr Lüding personally about his dessert? Thereupon the secretary, who sometimes travels with Mr Lüding to conferences and has lunch or dinner with him at some Palace or Inter Hotel or other, claims that when *she* is on a trip with him he invariably chooses *crème brûlée*. The cook: but this Sunday he wasn't going to be on a trip with her, the secretary, and mightn't Mr Lüding's choice of dessert depend on the society he happened to be in? Etc. Etc. Finally there was a long argument about crêpes with poppy seed – and this entire conversation is recorded on tape at the taxpayer's expense! And the person playing back the tape, who of course has to be on the lookout for an anarchist code in which crêpes might stand for hand grenades or strawberries and ice cream for bombs – does he think: The problems some people have! or: I wouldn't mind having such problems, for his daughter might just have run away from home or his son have taken to hash, or the rent might have gone up again, and all this – these tape recordings – merely because someone once uttered a bomb threat against Lüding. And this is how some innocent civil servant or employee finally finds out what crêpes with poppy seed are – someone for whom even one crêpe would do as a main meal.

Too much is happening in the foreground, and we know nothing about what is happening in the background. If only one could replay the tapes! To discover at last the degree of intimacy, if any, between Miss Else Woltersheim and Konrad Beiters. How much does 'friend' mean in terms of the relationship between these two? Does she call him Sweetheart, or Darling, or does she just say Konrad or Conny? What kind of verbal intimacies, if any, do they exchange? Does he sing to her over the phone – since he is known to have a good baritone voice, if not of concert at least of choral quality? Lieder? Serenades? Pop tunes? Operatic arias? Or might there even be crude itemizations of past or future intimacies? One would like to know, for most people, being denied reliable telepathic communication, reach for the phone, which they feel is more reliable. Do the authorities realize what they are asking of their employees in terms of the psyche? Let us assume that a temporarily suspect person of a vulgar nature, whose telephone is being officially tapped, calls up his equally vulgar sex partner of the moment. Since we live in a free country and may speak openly and frankly with one another, even over the phone, what sort of things may buzz in the ears of some moral, not to say moralistic, individual (regardless of sex) or come fluttering out of the tape? Can this be justified? Is there any provision for psychiatric treatment? What does the Union of Public Services, Transportation, and Communications say to *that*? There is concern for industrialists, anarchists, bank directors, bank robbers, and bank employees, but who is concerned about our national tape-security forces? Have the churches no comment to make on this? Has the Bishops' Conference at Fulda or the Executive Committee of German Catholics no ideas on the subject? Why does the Pope keep silent? Does no one realize all the things that assail innocent ears, ranging from *crème brûlée* to hardest porn? We see young people being encouraged to enter the civil service – and to what are they exposed? To moral outcasts of the telephone. Here at last we have an area where church and trade union might cooperate. Surely it should be possible to plan at least some kind of educational programme for telephone monitors? History lessons on tape? That shouldn't cost too much.

42

We now return contritely to the foreground, set to work on the inescapable channelling process – and must begin yet again with an explanation! We promised to let no more blood flow, and we wish to stress that, with the death of Mrs Blum, Katharina's mother, this promise has not been exactly broken. For this death, while not, of course, a normal one, was not a bloody murder. Mrs Blum's death was brought on by violence, true, but by unintentional violence. In any event – and this must be borne in mind – the person responsible for her death had no intention of committing murder, manslaughter, or even mayhem. The person concerned – and for this there is not only evidence but his own admission – was none other than Tötges, the very man who himself came to such a bloody end as the result of deliberate violence.

As early as Thursday, Tötges had inquired after and obtained Mrs Blum's address in Gemmelsbroich, but his attempts to get into the hospital to see her were unsuccessful. He was informed by the doorman, by Sister Edelgard, and by Dr Heinen, that Mrs Blum had just undergone a serious but successful cancer operation and was urgently in need of rest; that her recovery depended on not being exposed to any excitement whatever, and that an interview was out of the question. When reminded that, through her daughter's connection with Götten, Mrs Blum was also a 'public figure', the doctor countered with the remark that as far as he was concerned even public figures were first and foremost patients.

Now during this conversation Tötges had noticed that there were painters working in the building, and he later boasted to his colleagues that on Friday morning he succeeded, by using 'the simplest trick in the book, the workman trick', that is, by getting hold of some overalls, a paint pot, and a paint brush, in getting in to see Mrs Blum, for nothing was such a mine of information as a mother, even a sick one; he had, he said, confronted Mrs Blum with the facts but wasn't quite sure whether she understood all he said, for the name Götten obviously didn't ring a bell with her and she had said: 'Why did it have to end like this, why did it have to come to this?' out of which the *News* made: 'It

was bound to come to this, it was bound to end like this.'
Tötges accounted for the slight change in Mrs Blum's statement by saying that as a reporter he was used to 'helping
simple people to express themselves more clearly'.

43

It could not even be definitely established whether Tötges
actually had got to see Mrs Blum, or whether, in order to
present the words quoted in the *News* as having been spoken
by Katharina's mother in an interview, he had lied about or
invented his visit as an example of his one-upmanship and
efficiency as a reporter and to have something to boast about
as well. Dr Heinen, Sister Edelgard, a Spanish nurse called
Huelva, a Portuguese cleaning woman called Puelco – all
consider it out of the question that 'this fellow should actually have had the nerve to do such a thing' (Dr Heinen).
Now there is no doubt that the visit to Katharina's mother –
admitted although possibly invented – was of crucial importance, and the question naturally arises as to whether
the hospital staff is simply denying what ought not to have
happened, or whether Tötges, in order to authenticate the
words of Katharina's mother, invented the visit. We must
be scrupulously fair. There can be no doubt that it was *after*
Katharina had arranged the interview with Tötges and *after*
the *Sunday News* had published a further report by Tötges
that she made herself the Bedouin costume in order to do
some snooping in that very bar which the unfortunate
Schönner had left 'with some broad'. So we must wait and
see. One thing is certain, indeed confirmed, and that is that
Dr Heinen was surprised at the sudden death of his patient
Maria Blum and that he could not 'exclude the possibility

of unforeseen influences, despite the lack of evidence'. Innocent painters must not be saddled with the responsibility for this. The honour of the German craftsman must not be besmirched: neither Sister Edelgard nor the foreign ladies Huelva and Puelco can guarantee that all the painters – there were four of them, supplied by the firm of Merkens in Kuir – were in fact painters, and since all four were working in different parts of the building no one can be sure that someone in overalls and equipped with paint pot and brush did not sneak inside. The fact remains that Tötges *claimed* (the word 'admitted' should not be used, since there is no actual evidence of his visit) to have seen Maria Blum and to have interviewed her, and Katharina knew of this claim. Furthermore, Mr Merkens has admitted that of course not all of the four painters were present at the same time and that, *if* someone had wanted to sneak in, it would have been the simplest thing in the world. Dr Heinen said later that he would bring a charge against the *News* for publishing the alleged remark of Katharina's mother and create a scandal for, if it was true, it was monstrous – but his threat remained as unexecuted as the 'punch in the jaw' with which Blorna had threatened Sträubleder.

44

At about noon of that Saturday, 23 February 1974, the Blornas, Miss Woltersheim, Konrad Beiters, and Katharina finally all got together at the Café Kloog in Kuir, which was run by a nephew of the restaurant owners for whom Katharina had sometimes worked in the past, in the kitchen and as a waitress. Embraces were exchanged and tears were shed, even by Mrs Blorna. Needless to say, the customers at the café were in Carnival mood, but the proprietor, Erwin Kloog, an old and admiring friend of Katharina's, put his own living room at the disposal of the little group. From here, Blorna telephoned at once to Hach, cancelling the appointment for that afternoon in the museum lobby. He told Hach that Katharina's mother had died suddenly, probably as the result of a visit by Tötges from the *News*. Hach was more subdued than he had been that morning and asked Blorna to convey his personal sympathy to Katharina, who, he felt sure, bore him no grudge, and indeed why should she? Of course, he was at their disposal any time. Although he was very busy right now with the interrogation of Götten he would certainly find the time; incidentally, so far nothing had shown up in Götten's interrogation that could be damaging for Katharina. Götten had spoken of her with great affection and fairness. Permission for a visit, though, was not likely to be forthcoming since they were not related and the term 'fiancée' would almost certainly prove too vague to pass muster.

It looks very much as though Katharina was not exactly in a state of collapse following the news of her mother's death; it almost seems as though she was relieved. Of course Katharina showed Dr Heinen the edition of the *News* in which the Tötges interview was mentioned and her mother was quoted, but she certainly did not share Dr Heinen's indignation about the interview: on the contrary, she felt these people were murderers and character-assassins, and while naturally she despised them it was obviously the duty of that type of newspaper person to deprive the innocent of their honour, reputation, and health. Dr Heinen, mistakenly assuming her to be a Marxist (probably he too had read the insinuations of Brettloh, Katharina's divorced husband, in the *News*), was taken aback by her detachment and asked her whether she considered it – this *modus operandi* of the

News – to be a problem of the social structure. Katharina did not know what he meant, and shook her head.

She then followed Sister Edelgard to the mortuary, which she entered together with Miss Woltersheim. Katharina drew back the sheet from her mother's face with her own hands, said 'Yes', and kissed her on the forehead; when Sister Edelgard suggested Katharina say a short prayer, she shook her head and said 'No'. She replaced the sheet over her mother's face, thanked the nun, and only on leaving the mortuary did she start to cry, at first softly, then harder, then uncontrollably. Perhaps she was also thinking of her dead father whom, when she was a child of six, she had also seen for the last time in a hospital mortuary. Else Woltersheim remembered, or rather noted, that she had never seen Katharina cry before, not even as a child when she had been unhappy at school or because of her wretched environment. Very courteously, almost with a smile, Katharina insisted on thanking everyone, including the foreign ladies Huelva and Puelco, for all they had done for her mother. She left the hospital quite composed, nor did she forget to ask the hospital administration to send a telegram to the prison where her brother Kurt was confined so he might be informed.

That was how she remained the whole afternoon and throughout the evening: composed. Although again and again she took out the two issues of the *News* and confronted the Blornas, Else W., and Konrad B. with all the details and her interpretation of them, even her attitude towards the *News* seemed to have changed. In today's jargon: less emotional, more analytical. In this familiar and sympathetic circle of friends, in Erwin Kloog's living room, she also spoke of her relationship to Sträubleder: on one occasion he had brought her home after an evening at the Blornas and, although she had specifically and almost with revulsion told him not to, had accompanied her as far as her front door

91

and even into her apartment by simply placing his foot in the door. And then of course he had tried to make advances, probably had felt insulted because she had not found him at all irresistible, and finally – it was already close to midnight – had left. From then on he had positively persecuted her, and kept coming back, sending flowers, writing letters, on a few occasions had even managed to get into her apartment, and it was on one of those that he had simply forced the ring on her. That was all. That was why she had not admitted to his visits or revealed his name, because she had felt it would be impossible to explain to her interrogators that there had been nothing, absolutely nothing, not even a single kiss, between them. Who was going to believe that she would resist a man like Sträubleder, who was not only very well off but downright famous in the political, economic, and academic world for his irresistible charm, almost like a movie star; and who was going to believe of a woman like herself, a domestic, that she would resist a movie star, and not for moral reasons either but for reasons of taste? He had simply not had the slightest attraction for her, and she regarded this whole business of male visitors as the most horrible interference in a sphere which she would not like to call intimate since that would give the wrong impression and she had not been even remotely intimate with Sträubleder – but because he had got her into a situation that she could not explain to anyone, let alone a team of investigators. In the end, however – and here she laughed – she had felt grateful to him in a way, for the key to his house had been a big help to Ludwig, or at least the address, for – here she laughed again – Ludwig would certainly have got in without a key, but of course the key made it easier, and she had known too that the villa would be vacant during Carnival, for only two days before Sträubleder had once again made the worst possible nuisance of himself, positively forcing himself upon her and suggesting they spend a Carnival weekend together at the house before he had to leave for the conference at Bad B. in which he had agreed to take part. Yes, Ludwig had told her the police were looking for him, but he had merely said he was an army deserter and about to leave the country, and – she laughed for the third time – she had enjoyed personally dispatching him into the heating duct and telling him where the emergency exit was that led above ground at the end of 'Elegant Riverside Residences', at the corner of Hochkeppel-Strasse. No, she had not thought that she and Götten were being watched by the police, to her it had been a kind of cops and robbers affair, and it wasn't until next morning – Ludwig actually had left at six o'clock – that she had come to realize how serious the whole thing was. She registered relief that Götten had been arrested: now, she said, he wouldn't be able to do any more stupid things. She had been scared all the way through, there had been something downright weird about that Beizmenne.

45

At this juncture it must be noted that Saturday afternoon and evening passed quite pleasantly, so pleasantly that everyone – the Blornas, Else Woltersheim, and the strangely silent Konrad Beiters – felt almost reassured. Finally there was a general feeling – shared even by Katharina – that the 'situation had relaxed'. Götten arrested, Katharina's interrogation over, Katharina's mother released, albeit sooner than expected, from great suffering; funeral arrangements were already under way, all the necessary documents in Kuir promised for the Monday before Lent, an official having kindly declared his willingness to issue them that day although it was a holiday. And finally there was a certain consolation in the fact that the café proprietor Erwin Kloog, who would not hear of accepting payment for what had been consumed (i.e., coffee, liqueurs, potato salad, wieners, and cake), said as they left: 'Chin up, Katie, not all of us here think badly of you.' The consolation inherent in these words was perhaps only relative, for how much is 'not all' worth? Still, the fact remained that it was 'not all'. They agreed to drive to the Blornas and spend the rest of the evening there. On arrival, Katharina was strictly forbidden to take a hand, even her orderly one: she was on vacation and was told to relax. It was Miss Woltersheim who made some sandwiches in the kitchen while Blorna and Beiters together saw to the fire. And Katharina actually did let herself be 'spoiled for once'. Everything was really very nice, and if it had not been for a death and the arrest of a very dear person they would certainly have had a little impromptu dance in the small hours, for in spite of everything it was Carnival.

Blorna was unable to dissuade Katharina from the planned interview with Tötges. She remained calm and smiling, and later, after the interview – some 'interview'! Blorna felt his blood run cold at the recollection of the cool determination with which Katharina had insisted on the interview and how firmly she had declined his offer to be present. And yet, later, he was not quite sure whether Katharina had already decided on the murder that evening. It seemed to him much more likely that it had been triggered by the *Sunday News*.

They bade each other a peaceful good night, again with embraces, this time without tears, after listening to both serious and popular music together and after both Katharina and Else Woltersheim had told the others something about life in Gemmelsbroich and Kuir. It was barely half-past ten when Katharina, Miss Woltersheim, and Beiters parted from the Blornas with assurances of deep regard and fellow-feeling, and the Blornas congratulated themselves on having returned in time – in time to help Katharina – after all. Over the ashes in the fireplace and a bottle of wine, they discussed fresh vacation plans and the character of their friend Sträubleder and his wife Maud. When Blorna asked his wife to try not to use the phrase 'gentleman visitor' next time Sträubleder came, surely she must see how hypersensitive the term had become, Trude Blorna said: 'It'll be a while before we see *him* again.'

46

We can vouch for Katharina having spent the rest of the evening quietly. She tried on her Bedouin costume again, went over some of the seams, and decided to use a white handkerchief for a veil. They listened to the radio a while longer, ate some cookies, and then took themselves off to bed: Beiters going for the first time openly with Miss Woltersheim into her bedroom, and Katharina making herself comfortable on the sofa.

47

When Else Woltersheim and Konrad Beiters got up on Sunday morning, they found the breakfast table nicely prepared, the coffee decanted into the Thermos jug, and Katharina, who was already having her breakfast and clearly enjoying it, sitting at the living-room table reading the *Sunday News*. What follows is not so much comment as quotation. True,

Katharina's 'story' plus photo were no longer on the front page. This time the front page showed Ludwig Götten under the caption: 'Intimate partner of Katharina Blum takes cover in industrialist's villa. The story itself was in greater detail than before and appeared on pages 7 to 9 with numerous pictures: Katharina as a First Communicant, her father as a returning soldier, the church in Gemmelsbroich, once again the Blorna villa; Katharina's mother at about forty, careworn, almost worn out, standing outside the cottage in Gemmelsbroich where they used to live, and finally a picture of the hospital where Katharina's mother had died Friday night. The text ran as follows:

A victim of her own daughter: so may we describe the mother of Katharina Blum, that shadowy figure who is still at large, Mrs Blum not having survived the shock of being informed of her daughter's activities. While it is strange enough that, as her mother lay dying, the daughter should have been dancing at a ball in the tender embrace of a robber and murderer, it surely borders on the utmost perversity that she should have shed not a single tear at the news of her mother's death. Is this woman in truth merely 'ice-cold and calculating'? The wife of one of her former employers, a respected country doctor, describes her as follows: 'She behaved like a real little floozy. I had to let her go for the sake of my teenage sons, our patients, and my husband's reputation.' Is it possible that Katharina B. was involved in the embezzling activities of the notorious Fehnern? (The *News* published a complete report of that case at the time.) Was her father a malingerer? Why did her brother turn to crime? Still awaiting explanation are her rapid rise in the world and her substantial income.

It has now been definitely established that Katharina Blum provided Götten, the man with blood on his hands, with the means of escape; she shamelessly abused the affection, confidence, and spontaneous generosity of a highly respected professional man and industrialist. Information is now in the hands of the *News* proving almost conclusively that her activities consisted not in *receiving* male visitors but in making unsolicited visits of her own in order to 'case' the villa. Blum's 'mystery drives' are no longer so mysterious. Without a shred of scruple she gambled the reputation of an honourable man, the happiness of his family, and his political career (on which the *News* has published frequent reports), indifferent to the feelings of a loyal wife and four children. It would appear that Blum had been instructed by a Leftist group to destroy S.'s career.

Do the police and the public prosecutor's office really intend to believe the infamous Götten in his protestations of Blum's complete innocence in the affair? As so often in the past, once again the *News* raises the question: Can it be denied that our methods of interrogation are too mild? Are we to continue to treat with humanity those who commit inhuman acts?

Beneath the photos of Blorna, Mrs Blorna, and the villa:

It was in this house that Katharina Blum worked from seven a.m. to four-thirty p.m., on her own and unobserved, enjoying the full confidence of Dr and Mrs Blorna. What was going on here while the unsuspecting Blornas pursued their professions? Or were they not so unsuspecting after all? Their relationship with Blum is described as very cordial, almost familiar. Neighbours told reporters that it could almost be described as friendship. We will pass over certain insinuations since they are not relevant. Or are they? What was the role played by Mrs Gertrud Blorna, known to this day in the records of a respected technical college as 'Trude the Red'? How did Götten manage to escape from the Blum apartment although the police were on his heels? Who was familiar, down to the last detail, with the blueprints of the apartment complex known as 'Elegant Riverside Residences'? Mrs Blorna. Hertha Sch., sales clerk, and Claudia St., factory worker, made identical comments to the *News*: 'Those two, the way they danced together' (referring to Blum and the out-

97

law Götten) '– it was as if they'd known each other all their lives. That was no chance meeting, that was a reunion.'

48

When Beizmenne was later criticized by his colleagues for having left Götten unmolested for almost forty-eight hours, although his presence at the Sträubleder villa had been known to the police since 11.30 p.m. Thursday, thus risking another escape on the part of Götten, Beizmenne laughed, saying that ever since midnight Thursday Götten had had no further chance of escaping: the house was in the woods but, by great good luck, was surrounded by shooting blinds, 'as if by watchtowers'; the Minister for the Interior had been kept fully informed and had agreed to all the measures taken; a helicopter, which of course did not land within earshot, had put down a special detachment which was then deployed among the shooting blinds, and the following morning the local police force had been reinforced, very discreetly, by two dozen additional police officers. The main objective had been to observe Götten's attempts to make contact, and the success had justified the risk. Five contacts had been spotted, and of course it had first been necessary to pick up these five contacts and search their homes before arresting Götten. The police had waited to grab Götten until he had no further contacts to make and, out of either carelessness or bravado, had felt so safe that it had been possible to observe him from outside the villa.

Incidentally, there were certain important details for which he had to thank reporters from the *News* as well as the publishers of that paper and its affiliates that happened to have at their disposal more flexible and not always conventional methods of digging up information that had remained hidden from the investigating authorities. For example, Miss Woltersheim had turned out to be just as much of an unknown quantity as Mrs Blorna. Woltersheim had been born in 1930, the illegitimate child of a factory worker. The mother was still alive, and where do you suppose? In East Germany, and by no means against her will but voluntarily; she had frequently been invited to return to her native Kuir, where she owned a small house and an acre of land – the first time in 1945, again in 1952, yet again in 1961 shortly before the Berlin Wall went up. But she had refused – three times and all three times categorically. Of even greater interest was Woltersheim's father, a man called Lumm, likewise a factory worker and in addition a member of the then German Communist Party, and in 1932 he had emigrated to the Soviet Union, where he is said to have disappeared without trace. He – Beizmenne – supposed that this kind of missing person was not among those listed by the German Army as 'missing'.

49

There is always the possibility that certain relatively clear pointers towards a relationship between various events and actions will be misinterpreted or lost as mere hints; one further pointer should, therefore, be permitted: the *News*, which, of course, through its reporter Tötges was responsible for the unquestionably premature death of Katharina's mother, depicted Katharina in the *Sunday News* as being to blame for her mother's death and, moreover, accused her – more or less openly – of stealing Sträubleder's key to his country home! This point should be re-emphasized, for one can never be sure; nor quite sure whether one has fully realized to what extent the *News* has slandered, lied, and distorted.

Let us take Blorna as an example of the *extent* to which the *News* was able to affect comparatively rational people. We need hardly say that in the residential area where the Blornas lived no one bought the *Sunday News*. Reading tastes were loftier there. This explains how Blorna, who thought it was all over and was somewhat nervously awaiting the outcome of Katharina's conversation with Tötges, knew nothing about the article in the *Sunday News* until he called Miss Woltersheim. Miss Woltersheim, in turn, had taken it for granted that Blorna had already read the *Sunday News*. Now it is to be hoped that Blorna has been established as deeply and sincerely concerned for Katharina but also as a very level-headed person. On Miss Woltersheim now reading the relevant passages from the *Sunday News* aloud to him over the telephone, he could not – as they say – believe his ears. He asked her to read that again, after which he had not much choice but to believe it, and – as they say – he hit the roof. He shouted, roared, and rushed into the kitchen for an empty bottle, found one, ran off with it to the garage where, fortunately, he was intercepted by his wife and prevented from rigging up a Molotov cocktail that he intended to throw into the editorial offices of the *News*, to be followed by a second one into Sträubleder's town house. One must picture the scene: a man of forty-two, a university graduate, the object for the past seven years of Lüding's admiration and Sträubleder's respect for his sober, clear-headed negotiating abilities – and this on an international level, i.e., in Brazil, Saudi Arabia, and Northern Ireland, in other words not one of your provincial types but a thorough-going man of the world: *this* is the man who wanted to rig up a Molotov cocktail!

Mrs Blorna dismissed this instantly as spontaneous petit-bourgeois romantic anarchism, 'charmed away' his impulse the way one 'charms away' disease or pain from some part of the body, went to the telephone herself and had Miss Woltersheim read the relevant passages to her. It cannot be denied that she, even she, turned somewhat pale, and she did something that may have been worse than any Molotov cocktail: she reached for the phone, called Lüding (who happened to be enjoying his strawberries *with* whipped cream *plus* vanilla ice cream), and simply said to him: 'You bastard, you miserable little bastard!' She did not give her name, but it is safe to assume that all who knew the Blornas knew the voice of Mrs Blorna, who was notorious for the asperity and deadly aim of her remarks. This, in her husband's opinion, was in turn going too far: he thought she was calling Sträubleder. Well, the result was one row after another, between the Blornas, and between the Blornas and other people, but since nobody was killed we must be allowed to pass over them. We mention these trifling, even if deliberate, consequences of the *Sunday News* reporting merely to point out how even well-educated, well-established people can be so carried away by their indignation that they consider resorting to violence of the crudest kind.

It is known that at about this time – around noon – Katharina, after spending an hour and a half, unrecognized, at the reporters' hangout, presumably gathering information on Tötges, left the place known as the 'Golden Duck' and was waiting in her apartment for Tötges, who appeared some fifteen minutes later. We assume there is no more to be said concerning the 'interview'. The outcome is known. (See page 9.)

50

In order to check the truth of the statement made by the Gemmelsbroich pastor – a statement that had surprised *everyone* involved – that Katharina's father had been a Communist in disguise, Blorna drove out to the village, where he spent a day. First of all: the pastor confirmed his statement, saying that the *News* had quoted him correctly and word for word, no, he could offer no proof of his claim nor did he want to, he even said he did not *need* to, he could still rely on his sense of smell and he had simply smelled that Blum was a Communist. When asked to define his sense of smell he refused, nor was he very helpful when Blorna then asked him kindly to explain, if he could not define his sense of smell, *what* the smell of a Communist was like, *how* a Communist smelled, and at this point – it has to be said – the pastor became quite rude, asked Blorna whether he was a Catholic and, when Blorna said yes, reminded him of his duty to be obedient, which Blorna did not understand. From then on, he ran into difficulties over his inquiries concerning the Blums, who did not appear to have been especially popular; he heard bad things about Katharina's deceased mother, who had indeed finished *one* bottle of sacramental wine in the sacristy with the help of the verger (since dismissed); he heard bad things about Katharina's brother, who had been a regular nuisance, but the only words of Katharina's father to substantiate his Communism were a remark he made in 1949 to Scheumel, a farmer, in one of the seven village taverns, and this was supposed to have been: 'There are worse things than Socialism.' That was all he could glean. The only result for Blorna was that, at the conclusion of his inquiries in the village, he was himself described, if not precisely abused, as a Communist, and that came (something he found particularly painful) from a woman who until then had been quite helpful and had even displayed a certain sympathy towards him: the retired schoolteacher Elma Zubringer who, as he said good-bye, gave him a mocking smile, even a bit of a wink, saying: 'Why don't you admit that you're one of them too – and your wife most of all?'

51

Unfortunately we cannot ignore one or two acts of violence that occurred while Blorna was preparing for the trial of Katharina. His greatest mistake was in acceding to Katharina's request to take over Götten's defence as well, and in repeatedly trying to obtain permission for the two to visit each other, insisting that they were engaged. It was, he maintained, in the course of that very evening, 20 February, and of the ensuing night that the engagement had taken place. Etc. Etc. It is not hard to imagine the kind of thing the *News* wrote about him, about Götten and Katharina, about Mrs Blorna. We do not intend to cite each instance here. Certain infringements of or departures from the level are to be undertaken only when necessary, and here they are not necessary because by this time the reader must know what to expect from the *News*. The rumour was being circulated that Blorna wanted a divorce, a rumour without a grain of truth to it but which nevertheless sowed the seeds of mistrust between husband and wife. It was claimed that he was in financial straits, which was bad because it was true. The fact was that he had somewhat overextended himself in assuming a kind of custodianship for Katharina's apartment, which was almost impossible to rent or sell because it was considered 'bloodstained'. Anyway, it dropped in value, yet Blorna had to continue the payments for amortization, interest, etc., in unreduced amounts. In fact there was already some indication that Haftex, the owners of 'Elegant Riverside Residences', were considering suing Katharina Blum for damages, claiming that she had impaired the rental, commercial, and social value of their apartment complex. We see then: trouble, quite a lot of trouble. An application to the courts for permission to dismiss Mrs Blorna from the architectural firm on grounds of breach of confidence (i.e., familiarizing Katharina with the substructure of the apartment complex) was turned down, but nobody is sure which way the appeal courts will decide. One more thing: the Blornas have already got rid of their second car, and recently there was a picture in the *News* of the Blorna limousine, which really is rather elegant, over the caption: 'When will the "red" attorney have to switch to the average man's car?'

52

Need we say that Blorna's association with Lüstra has been affected if not dissolved? The only matters still under discussion now are the 'winding up' of certain transactions. However, he was recently informed by Sträubleder over the telephone: 'We're not going to let you and Trude starve,' and what surprised Blorna in this was Sträubleder's inclusion of Trude. He still acts on behalf of Lüstra and Haftex but no longer at the international or even the national level, only rarely at the regional and mostly at the local level. In other words, he has to grapple with petty defaulters and troublemakers who submit claims for the promised marble panelling when the walls have been faced with mere green slate; or types who, when they have been promised three coats of enamel on their bathroom doors, scrape off the paint with a knife and hire experts to confirm that there are only two coats. Then there are the dripping faucets and defective garbage disposals used as a pretext for withholding contractual payments – this is the kind of case now being dumped in his lap, whereas he used to be flying continually if not continuously, between Buenos Aires and Persepolis to take part in plans for major projects. In the army this is known as a demotion, a process usually associated with some degree of humiliation. Result: no stomach ulcers yet, but Blorna's stomach is beginning to complain.

It was unfortunate that he made his own inquiries in Kohlforstenheim with a view to finding out from the local chief of police whether the key had been on the inside or the outside of the door at the time of Götten's arrest, or whether there had been any sign of Götten having broken in. Why bother, now that the inquiries have all been completed? This – there is no denying – is no way to cure stomach ulcers, for all that Police Chief Hermanns was very nice to him, and yet, far from accusing him of Communism, he did strongly urge him not to interfere. There is one consolation for Blorna: his wife is being nicer to him all the time, and although she still has a sharp tongue she now reserves it for use against others (although not against all others) instead of against him. So far the only obstacle to her plan of selling the villa and buying Katharina's apartment for themselves is the size of the apartment: it is too small, for Blorna wants to give up his town office and wind up any outstanding business at home. Blorna, who used to be known as liberal-minded and a *bon vivant*, a popular, jovial colleague who gave wonderful parties, is beginning to take on the air of an ascetic and to neglect his appearance, to which he had always attached great importance; and because he is *genuinely* neglecting it, not just as a fad, some of his colleagues are even saying that he is overlooking the most basic personal hygiene and no longer smells as he should. Hence there is little reason to hope for a new career for him, the fact being (nothing, nothing whatever, must be withheld) that his body no longer smells at it used to, i.e., like that of a man who every morning jumps into the shower and uses plenty of soap, deodorant, and toilet water. In short: a considerable change is taking place in him. His friends – he still has a few, among them Hach, with whom he happens to be professionally involved in the Götten and Blum cases – are seriously concerned, especially since his aggressions – e.g., vis-à-vis the *News*, which still remembers him from time to time with short items – no longer explode but are quite obviously being swallowed. His friends' concern is such that they have asked Trude Blorna to check discreetly whether Blorna is acquiring any weapons or concocting explosives, for the murdered Tötges has a successor who, under the name of Eginhard Templer, is carrying on a kind of continuation of Tötges; this Templer managed to photograph Blorna just as the latter was entering a pawnshop; then, by photographing through the window, he was able to offer readers of the *News* a view of Blorna negotiating with the pawnbroker: under discussion was the loan value of a ring being scrutinized by the pawnbroker through a jeweller's loupe. Caption: 'Have the "red" sources really dried up, or is someone faking financial distress?'

53

Blorna's chief concern is to persuade Katharina to testify at the actual trial that she did not make the decision to take revenge on Tötges until the Sunday morning, and that her intention had been not to kill him but to scare him off. She was to say that, although on the Saturday, when she invited Tötges to an interview, she had meant to tell him what she thought of him in no uncertain terms and to point out what he had done to her life and her mother's life, she had not wanted to kill him even on the Sunday, even after reading the article in the *Sunday News*. He felt it was imperative to avoid the impression that Katharina had planned the murder for several days and had proceeded according to plan. Although she claims to have *thought about* murder on Thursday after reading the first article, he tried to make her realize that many people – including himself – occasionally do think about murder but that one must distinguish between thinking about murder and planning a murder.

Another thing worrying Blorna is that Katharina is still showing no signs of remorse, which means that she will not be able to show any in court. She is not at all depressed: on the contrary, she seems quite happy because she is living 'under the same conditions as my dear Ludwig'. She is considered a model prisoner, works in the kitchen but, if the opening of the trial is further delayed, is to be transferred to the commissary where, however (so one hears), she is most unenthusiastically awaited: there is dismay on the part of both administration and inmates at the reputation for integrity that precedes her, and the prospect of Katharina spending her entire prison term working within the commissary system (it is predicted that a sentence of fifteen years will be asked for and that she will get eight to ten) is spreading alarm through every prison in the country. Thus we see that integrity, combined with intelligent organizing ability, is not desired anywhere, not even in prisons, and not even by the administration.

54

As Hach informed Blorna in confidence, the murder charge against Götten is not likely to stand up and will therefore be dropped. The fact that he not only deserted from the army but also acted to the considerable detriment (both moral and material) of this hallowed institution is regarded as proven. His crime was not bank robbery but the total cleaning out of a safe that had contained the pay for two regiments as well as substantial cash reserves; also falsifying the accounts and theft of a weapon. Well, a sentence of eight to ten years is expected for him too. This means that when released he would be about thirty-four and Katharina about thirty-five, and she really does have plans for the future: she calculates that by the time she is released interest will have increased her capital substantially, and when the time comes she intends to open, 'somewhere, not here of course', a 'restaurant with outside catering service'. Permission to consider herself Götten's fiancée will probably be decided at the highest, not merely a higher, level. The relevant applications have been submitted and are already on their long march from one department to another. Incidentally, the telephone contacts made by Götten from Sträubleder's country house were all to members of the army or their wives, including officers and officers' wives. A scandal of moderate dimensions is predicted.

55

While Katharina, restricted only in her freedom, is looking almost untroubled to the future, Else Woltersheim is on the way to a state of steadily increasing bitterness. She was extremely upset at the defamation of her mother and her deceased father, who is regarded as a victim of Stalinism. There are indications in Else Woltersheim of intensified antisocial tendencies which not even Konrad Beiters is able to alleviate. Since Else is now specializing more and more in cold buffets, i.e., in organizing, supplying, and supervising them, her aggressiveness is being increasingly directed at the guests, whether foreign or domestic journalists, industrialists, trade-union officials, bankers, or junior executives. 'Sometimes,' she told Blorna not long ago, 'I have to force myself not to throw a bowl of potato salad over the tuxedo of some moron or a plate of smoked salmon down the cleavage of some stupid cow, just to see them shudder for once. Try and imagine the picture from our side: how they stand there with their mouths wide open and their tongues hanging out and how of course they all make a dash for the caviar canapés – and there are some who I know are millionaires, or the wives of millionaires, who even stuff their pockets and purses with cigarettes and matches and petits fours. Soon they'll be bringing along plastic containers to carry away the coffee – and all that, every bit of it, is being paid for one way or another out of our taxes. There are characters who go without breakfast or lunch so they can fall like vultures on a cold buffet – not that I mean to insult vultures.'

56

So far we know of only one instance of an actual exchange of blows, one which unfortunately aroused a good deal of public attention. It was at the preview of the exhibition of the work of the painter Frederick Le Boche, whose patron Blorna is considered to be, that Blorna and Sträubleder came face to face again for the first time. As Sträubleder approached him with a broad grin, Blorna did not hold out his hand, but this did not prevent Sträubleder from grabbing it and whispering: 'For God's sake, don't take it all so seriously! We're not going to let you and Trude go to the dogs – you're the one who's doing that.' Well, if we are to be honest we have regretfully to report that at this moment Blorna did punch Sträubleder in the jaw. Without further ado, so that it may be forgotten without further ado: blood flowed, from Sträubleder's nose; according to private estimates, some four to seven drops but, what was worse: although Sträubleder backed away he did say: 'I forgive you, I forgive you everything – considering your emotional state.' And so it was that this remark apparently maddened Blorna, provoking something described by witnesses as a 'scuffle', and, as is usually the case when the Sträubleders and Blornas of this world show themselves in public, a *News* photographer by the name of Kottensehl (successor to the murdered Schönner) was present, and we can hardly be shocked at the *News* (its nature being now known) for publishing the photograph of this scuffle under the heading: 'Conservative politician assaulted by Leftist attorney.' Not until the following morning, of course.

At the exhibition there was furthermore a confrontation between Maud Sträubleder and Trude Blorna. Maud

Sträubleder said to Trude Blorna: 'I do sympathize with you so, Trude dear,' whereupon Trude B. said to Maud S.: 'You can put your sympathy right back in the fridge where you keep all the rest of your feelings.' Upon Maud offering her forgiveness, indulgence, pity, indeed almost love, with the words: 'Nothing, nothing, not even your destructive remarks, can lessen my sympathy,' Trude B. replied in words that cannot be repeated here, only noted; ladylike is not the way to describe the words in which Trude B. hinted at Sträubleder's numerous advances to her and, among other things – thus violating the professional secrecy to which even the wife of an attorney is bound – alluded to the ring, the letters, and key which 'your consistently rejected suitor left behind in a certain apartment.' At this point the squabbling ladies were parted by Frederick Le Boche, who with great presence of mind had seized upon the chance to catch Sträubleder's blood on a piece of blotting paper and had converted it into what he called 'a specimen of instant art'. This he entitled 'End of a Long Friendship', signed, and gave not to Sträubleder but to Blorna, saying: 'Here's something you can peddle to help you out of a hole.' From this occurrence plus the preceding acts of violence it should be possible to deduce that Art still has a social function.

57

It is indeed deplorable that here, as we approach the conclusion, there should be so little harmony to report and but slight hope of any in the future. The outcome has been not integration but confrontation. Naturally the question must arise: *Why?* Here is a young woman, cheerfully, almost gaily, going off to a harmless little private dance, and four days later she becomes (since this is merely a report, not a judgement, we will confine ourselves to facts) a murderess, and this, if we examine the matter closely, because of newspaper reports. We see quarrels and tensions and finally scuffles arising between two men who have been friends for a very, very long time. Pointed remarks made by their wives. Rejected sympathy, in fact rejected love. Highly unpleasant developments. A genial, broad-minded man, who loves life, travel, luxury, neglects himself so seriously that he emits body odour! He has even been found to have bad breath. He puts his house up for sale, he goes to the pawnbroker. His wife is looking around 'for another job' since she is convinced that her firm's second application for dismissal will go against her; she is even prepared – this talented woman is prepared – to work as little better than a sales clerk (with the title 'Interior Decorating Consultant') for one of the large furniture outfits, but there she is told 'that the circles in which we are accustomed to do business are precisely those, Madam, where you have made enemies.'

In short: things do not look good. Hach, the public prosecutor, has already been whispering to friends something that he has not yet had the courage to tell Blorna: that Blorna may be turned down as defence counsel on grounds of his undue involvement. What will happen, how will it end? What will happen to Blorna if he can no longer visit Katharina and – it has to come out! – hold hands with her? There is no doubt about it: he loves her, she does not love him, and he hasn't a hope in the world, since everything, everything, belongs to her 'dear Ludwig'! And we must add that this 'holding hands' is a purely one-sided affair, for all it consists of is that, when Katharina passes files or notes or papers across to him, he places his hands on hers for longer – perhaps three, four, at most five tenths of a second longer – than is customary. How in the world are we to bring about harmony here, when not even his strong attachment to Katharina prompts him to, let us say, wash a bit more often? Not even the fact that he, he alone, discovered the origin of the murder weapon – where Biezmenne, Moeding, and their assistants had failed – was any comfort to him. Perhaps it is too much to say 'discovered': what actually happened was that Konrad Beiters voluntarily admitted to having once been a Nazi and that this alone explained why so far no one had paid any attention to him. It was true, he had been Party leader in Kuir and at the time had been able to do something for Miss Woltersheim's mother, and, well, the pistol was an old service one that he had kept hidden but stupidly enough occasionally shown to Else and Katharina; the three of them had once even gone out into the woods for some target practice; Katharina had turned out to be a good shot and had told him that as a girl she had worked as a waitress at Rifle Club meetings and had sometimes been allowed to fire a few rounds. Well, on the Saturday evening Katharina had asked him for the key to his apartment, saying she hoped he would understand, she just wanted to be alone for a while, her own apartment was dead for her, dead – yet that Saturday night she had stayed with Else so she must have picked up the pistol from his apartment on the Sunday, it must have been after breakfast and after reading the *Sunday News*, when she had driven off in her Bedouin costume to that reporters' hangout.

58

But finally we do have something reasonably cheerful to report: Katharina told Blorna the whole story; she also told him how she had spent the six or seven hours between the murder and her appearance at Moeding's home. We are in the fortunate position of being able to quote. Fortunately, this account can be quoted verbatim, Katharina having written it all down and given Blorna permission to use it at the trial.

The only reason I went to that reporters' bar was to have a look at him. I wanted to know what that kind of man looked like, what his movements were like, how he talked, drank, danced – that man who had destroyed my life. Yes, I did go first to Konrad's apartment to pick up the pistol, I even loaded it myself. I had asked him to show me how, that time we did some target practice in the woods.

I waited in the bar for an hour and a half, maybe two hours, but he didn't show up. I had decided that, if he was too awful, I wouldn't even go to the interview, and it's true – if I had seen him before I wouldn't have gone. But he never came to the bar. To avoid being pestered, I asked the landlord – his name is Peter Kraffluhn, I know him from the extra jobs I take on, where he sometimes helps out as head waiter – I asked him to let me help serve behind the bar. Of course Peter knew what the *News* had been saying about me, he had promised to give me the high sign if Tötges turned up. Seeing it was Carnival, I didn't mind being asked to dance a few times, but when Tötges failed to show up I must say I got very nervous, I didn't want to meet with him cold.

So at noon I drove home, and I felt terrible in that stained and soiled apartment. I only had to wait a few minutes before the bell rang, just enough time to release the safety catch on the pistol and slip it into my handbag ready to pull out. And then the bell rang, and there he was outside the door when I opened it, and here I'd been thinking he had pressed it downstairs and I would have a few extra minutes, but he had already come up in the elevator, and there he was, standing right in front of me, and it was a shock. Well, I could see right away what a bastard he was, a real bastard. And good-looking, too. What people call good-looking. Anyway, you've seen his pictures. He said: 'Well, Blumikins, what'll we do now, you and me?' I didn't say a word, just stepped back into the living room, and he followed me in, saying: 'Why do you look at me like that, Blumikins, as if you're scared out of your wits? How about us having a bang for a start?' Well, by this time I had my hand in my purse, and as he went for my dress I thought: 'Bang, if that's what you want,' and I pulled out the pistol and shot him then and there. Twice, three times, four times – I don't remember exactly. The police report will tell you how many times. Now I don't want you to think this was something new for me, a man going for my dress – when you've worked in other people's homes ever since you were fourteen, and even earlier, you're used to that. But *this* fellow – and then 'a bang'! and I thought: O.K., bang away. Of course he hadn't counted on that, and for a split second he looked at me in amazement, like in the movies when someone gets shot out of a clear blue sky. Then he fell to the floor, and I think he was dead. I threw the pistol down beside him and fled, down in the elevator and back to the bar, and Peter was astonished, since I'd been gone hardly half an hour. I went on working at the bar but I didn't dance any more, and all the time I was thinking, 'It can't be true,' but I knew it was true. And now and again Peter would come up and say: 'He's not going to show today, that boyfriend of yours,' and I would say: 'Doesn't look like it.' And behave as if I didn't care. Until four o'clock I poured schnapps and drew beer and opened champagne bottles and served snacks. Then I left, without saying good-bye to Peter. First I went into a church next door and sat there for maybe half an hour thinking about my mother and the wretched miserable life she had had, and about my father too, who was always grumbling, always

always, and cursing the government and the church and the civil service, and officers and everything, but whenever he had anything to do with any of them he would crawl, almost whimper, as he grovelled. And I thought about my husband, Brettloh, and about those rotten lies he told Tötges, and of course about my brother, who was for ever after my money the minute I'd earned a few marks and managed to squeeze it out of me for some nonsense or other, like clothes or motorbikes or gambling, and of course about the pastor, who in school always used to call me 'our pink Katie', and I didn't know what he meant, and the whole class would laugh because then I really would turn pink. Yes. And of course about Ludwig. Then I left the church and went to the nearest movie, and left the movie again, and went into another church, because on that Carnival Sunday it was the only place where a person could find a bit of peace. And of course I thought about the dead man back there in my apartment. Without remorse, without regret. He had wanted a bang, hadn't he, and I'd banged, hadn't I? And for a moment I thought it was the fellow who used to ring me up at night and who had pestered poor Else too. I thought: that's his voice all right, and I wanted to let him rattle on for a bit, to be quite sure, but what good would that have done me? And then I suddenly longed for some strong coffee and went to the Café Bekering, not to the restaurant but to the kitchen, because I knew Käthe Bekering, the owner's wife, from home-ec school. Käthe was very kind to me, although she was pretty busy. She gave me a cup of her own coffee, the kind Grandma used to make by pouring boiling water on to the ground coffee. But then she began talking about that stuff in the *News*, quite nicely yet somehow in a way that made me feel she believed at least a bit of it – and anyway how are people to know that it's all lies? I tried to explain to her, but she didn't understand, she just winked at me and said, 'So you really love this fellow?' and I said, 'Yes.' And then I thanked her for the coffee, and when I got outside I took a cab and drove to see Moeding, the police officer who had been so nice to me before.

Translator's Acknowledgement

I am deeply grateful to my husband, William
Vennewitz, for the patient and knowledgeable
assistance he has given me in the translation of
this book.

Leila Vennewitz

More About Penguins
and Pelicans